Jake the Time Jumper

The Portal Walker, Book 1

A.D. Tenebris

RWCM, LLC

Third book edition: January 24, 2026

ISBN: 979-8-218-86698-3

Published by RWCM, LLC. All rights reserved.

Contents

Chapter 1: Code Red

Jake Parker sat at his cluttered desk, tapping an erratic rhythm on the worn wooden surface as his gaze drifted to the ceiling. His fingers hovered over the keyboard, eager to begin their familiar dance. The computer's blue light cast an otherworldly glow, illuminating the organized chaos of his room. Circuit board tapestries hung above his bed like a shrine to technology, while posters of Ada Lovelace and Steve Jobs watched silently over each keystroke.

He shook his head, snapping back to focus. His latest project—a small but intricate program—was nearly complete. The clicking resumed, filling the room with a symphony of anticipation. Each line of code became a brushstroke in a digital masterpiece only he could envision. The gentle hum of the computer acted like a heartbeat, urging him toward the finish.

Then, silence.

Jake hit Enter.

The room held its breath with him. A single ping echoed from the machine—clean, triumphant. He didn't blink. Not yet. The program had executed successfully: a virtual applause in a cheerful note. Pride surged in his chest, the thrill of creation coursing through him like electricity. He tapped his portable coding rig to update the script library. It was a modular device still in development, but brimming with potential.

"How does it feel to be a genius?" he mused aloud, startled by the sound of his own voice. He chuckled softly, as if sharing a private joke with the silent icons on his wall. Maybe he was. Those pioneers knew the exhilaration of bending the digital world to their will.

Jake swiveled in his chair, taking in the tangled wires and brightly colored coding books that made up his sanctuary. Out there, he was Jake Parker, high school sophomore—just another kid navigating essays, exams, cafeteria awkwardness, and the occasional mockery. But here, he was Jake the creator, the inventor. A maestro conducting an orchestra of ones and zeroes.

Reflecting on his journey, Jake remembered his first encounter with code. Middle school, a classroom lined with dated computers. He was just another kid until he saw the potential—an entire universe awaiting within those flickering screens. From his first humble game, "Maze Runner," to his latest triumph, "Mindy," each project was a testament to his growing mastery and relentless curiosity. The room seemed to whisper their stories, each gadget and book a chapter in his personal odyssey.

"Dinner in five!" His mother's call drifted up the staircase, preceding the inevitable bustle of family life. The interruption tugged him briefly from his reverie, his thoughts lingering nonetheless on his next potential conquest, the next code that would defy boundaries.

A door creaked open behind him. Emma, his younger sister, leaned against the frame, a grin spreading as she surveyed the organized chaos.

"Did the world just get another one of Jake's masterpieces?"

"Finished it just now," he said, spinning in his chair. "Pretty sure it's my best yet."

Her eyes widened in admiration. "Are you going to show me or keep it secret like last time? That was totally unfair. I'm still wondering what 'Mindy' even does."

"I might show you," Jake teased, ruffling her hair as she ducked away. "If you can handle the awesomeness."

Emma rolled her eyes, but the intrigue lingered. "Just wait until you need my artistic touch to pretty up your next big thing. Then we'll see who's awesome."

He turned back to the computer, her quiet admiration fueling something deeper. Their bond—occasional but genuine—always gave him pause.

"Hey," he added, half to himself. "I think I'm... close to something. Like, actually close."

Emma stepped forward, resting a hand on his shoulder. "You know, even if I'm not coding at your speed, I can still keep up when I need to. My ideas find their own path," she said with a playful glint. "So no robot sisters—I'm one of a kind."

Jake laughed. "Don't worry. I'll make sure to code in your quirks. No one could replace that."

He glanced around his room once more, letting the calm linger before the next wave of ideas hit. Each project was more than just code—it was a beacon, a way forward through the stormy seas of adolescence.

Downstairs, the scent of roasted chicken and thyme drifted up, calling him back to reality. His mom's voice followed.

"Jake! Emma! Dinner's ready!"

He hesitated, then stood, the blue glow from his monitor blending with twilight like a second sunset. Each step down the creaking stairs pulled him from his thoughts—out of loops and logic and into the rhythms of family life.

The door to his room creaked behind him.

But it never quite clicked shut.

Moments later, Emma slipped quietly into the hallway, moving like sound might wake something. She glanced toward the stairs, listening for the clink of plates, then turned back to the faint light spilling from Jake's room. The rig's LEDs blinked in a steady diagnostic rhythm.

Emma hesitated.

Then stepped inside.

Her hoodie sleeves hung long past her wrists like they always did, but the leather cord at her neck was new. It caught on the fabric as she moved. A round pendant pressed against her collarbone—smooth stone, coin-sized, deep azure. The markings etched into it were delicate and wrong in a way she couldn't explain: overlapping spirals like a maze, except the lines seemed to rearrange if you stared too long. Not shifting. Not moving. Just... refusing to settle into one shape.

She didn't like people touching it. She didn't like people asking about it.

Jake had forgotten she even had it.

She'd found it at a flea market last Christmas, on a day that should've been ordinary.

It hadn't felt ordinary.

The market had been packed: folding tables, old toys, chipped mugs, boxes of vinyl that smelled like basements. She'd only drifted from her parents for a minute, chasing nothing in particular, when she spotted the stall. Plain. Unmarked. The trinkets laid out too precisely.

And behind it, an old woman.

Not "sweet old lady" old.

Not a sweet old lady—weathered. Her coat was too thin for December. Her gloves looked made for chemicals, not cash. Her eyes latched onto Emma like she was checking off a list.

Emma had stopped without knowing why.

The pendant sat near the edge of the table as if it had been placed there on purpose. No price tag. No velvet display. Just stone on cheap fabric, like it didn't belong anywhere else.

Emma reached out.

The woman's hand moved just enough to slide the pendant closer. An invitation. Not pressure. More like... permission.

"Is this yours?" Emma asked.

The old woman's mouth twitched, almost a smile. "It's yours if you take it," she said, voice dry as paper.

"How much?"

"Nothing," the woman replied immediately.

Emma frowned. "Everything costs something."

The woman's gaze shifted—past Emma's shoulder, across the crowd, then returned. "Not today."

Emma picked up the cord. The stone was colder than it should've been. Heavier than it looked.

The woman leaned forward, close enough that Emma caught the faint scent of antiseptic and smoke. "Don't wait for someone else to choose it for you," she said quietly.

Emma swallowed. "Why?"

For a heartbeat, the woman looked tired. Not old. Tired. Like time itself had worn thin.

She pressed a folded bill into Emma's palm—change Emma hadn't asked for, from money she hadn't offered.

Then, a shift. The woman's eyes softened. Not with kindness. With relief.

By the time Emma blinked and turned to call her mom, the stall looked the same... except it wasn't a stall anymore. Just empty space between two tables, like it had never been there at all.

Emma stood holding the pendant, heart pounding, wondering if she'd imagined it all.

She hadn't.

Now, in Jake's room, the pendant shifted against her skin—subtle, like a tug on the cord. Not painful. Just present.

Emma's eyes drifted to the rig.

Jake's Bridge sat beside the keyboard, LEDs blinking steady, quiet. A command window remained open on the monitor: lines of code paused mid-thought, frozen like a sentence that didn't know how to end.

She didn't understand the code—nested functions, variables named like inside jokes—but its shape made her uneasy. There was intention. Structure.

She stepped closer.

The rig emitted a soft chirp.

Emma froze.

The pendant warmed—slow and deliberate, like breath against skin. Then a pulse—not frightening. Just... aware.

The rig blinked again, timed with the pendant.

Emma's breath snagged. She didn't touch anything. She didn't need to.

The monitor glitched once, too fast to read.

Then it was gone, replaced by Jake's paused code like nothing happened.

Emma stepped back.

The warmth vanished, like whatever had reached out had chosen to wait.

She stared at the rig, suddenly sure she was standing too close to something she didn't understand.

What are you building, Jake?

She turned and left quickly, feet soft on the stairs, heart tapping out a tight, sharp staccato.

At dinner, she smiled when she was supposed to. Laughed in the right places. Teased Dad forgetting gas.

But her hand kept drifting—unconsciously—to the pendant.

Each time she touched it, she felt the lingering warmth.

Whatever Jake was working on…

It wasn't just code anymore.

It had noticed her.

The dining room glowed with warm light. The round oak table was set with its usual mix of chipped plates and comfort food. Jake's parents, seated under the chandelier's soft glow, greeted him with familiar smiles—weathered but steady pillars of his world.

Emma bounced in her chair, feet barely grazing the floor, eyes bright with an energy that contrasted Jake's quiet demeanor.

"What are you working on now, Jake?" she asked lightly, though her curiosity ran deeper than her tone suggested.

Jake smirked, slipping into his usual mix of humility and bravado. "Just an app to organize school chaos. Nothing world-ending."

Emma laughed, but it didn't quite reach her eyes.

She was still thinking about the rig. About the blinking light. About the code that had stuttered and vanished.

"Must be pretty complex," she murmured.

Jake raised an eyebrow. "You okay?"

Emma blinked. "Yeah. Just thinking."

Their parents exchanged a glance—a subtle, well-practiced dance. Their father, a hardware engineer more comfortable with machines than mystery, nodded proudly.

"That's impressive, son," he said, voice thick with genuine pride even if the tech specifics escaped him.

His mother added with a chuckle, "Just make sure your app reminds you to feed Emma's cats."

Emma giggled, and Jake joined in. Their shared look said more than words—a sibling code-switch between teasing and understanding.

Still, beneath the humor, a gap lingered. They celebrated Jake's wins without knowing their weight. His projects were sparks to them—bright and impressive. But to Jake, they were something deeper.

He smiled, grateful yet restless.

"I'm thinking about something bigger. Something... extraordinary."

His father leaned forward, curiosity overtaking comprehension. "Extraordinary? Well, whatever it is, you've got us behind you. Even if I still don't understand your mom's grocery apps."

Emma giggled again, dispelling the brief weight in the room.

Dinner continued—questions, laughter, stories passed like side dishes. These were the rituals that tethered him. Even if his dreams spoke in algorithms, these moments translated into belonging.

Emma teased, "Think your app can remind Dad to get gas this time?"

"Oh, I've got enough reminders already," Dad replied, nudging his wife with a grin.

"And one for me—so I don't burn dessert," Mom added.

Their voices wove a soft web of comfort around the table.

Jake listened, laughed, responded. But part of him still stood on the edge—longing to merge the vastness of his ambitions with the warmth of this circle. His dreams stretched far beyond this room, but their love grounded him.

In that tension—between bytes and belonging—he found both his hunger and his hope.

The next day, Jake moved through the polished hallways of Waltham High, his sneakers whispering over the linoleum. Students rushed past in a blur of voices and footsteps, their eyes glued to glowing tablets. Jake wove through the chaos with calm.

Waltham High had embraced tech like a second skin. Electronic notice boards blinked with updates; digital lockers chimed softly as students tapped codes. The entire place pulsed with invisible Wi-Fi threads binding together its mechanical heartbeat.

Jake thrived in this network. He wasn't just a student—he was the unofficial tech whisperer. When devices failed, when code crashed, when someone needed a system untangled, Jake was the first call.

And yet, he preferred machines. They followed logic. They made sense. Unlike conversations.

As he walked, a student appeared at his elbow. "Hey, Jake, my tablet's being weird again. Can you take a look?"

Jake paused, turning with a friendly grin. "Sure, let me see."

He deftly toggled through the settings, fingers dancing across the screen like he was playing a well-rehearsed piano piece. Within moments, the problem was solved. The student offered a grateful grin and rushed off.

Jake continued on, passing familiar faces and half-heard greetings until he reached the computer lab. Here, keys clicked in rhythm, and hushed voices whispered over lines of code.

"Jake, could you help out with something?"

Another voice. Another screen. Another fix.

His day unfolded like this: a quiet loop of tech and tasks. Somewhere between classes, Liam appeared with a grin and a few of his usual crew in tow.

"Yo, Code Lord," Liam said, falling in step beside him. "How many spells did it take to resurrect Thompson's presentation?"

Jake smirked. "Just two incantations and a blood sacrifice."

"Classic. You running a dark arts side hustle yet?"

"Only for premium clients. You couldn't afford me."

Liam scoffed. "Please. I pay you in eternal praise."

Jake raised an eyebrow. "I'd prefer pizza."

"You and your tech rituals, man," Liam said, half-laughing. "One day, that keyboard's gonna open a portal to hell."

Jake's smile twitched. "Wouldn't be the worst place to test a new interface."

The others joined in the banter, their voices overlapping like audio tracks, building a casual rhythm.

Their camaraderie was its own kind of code—half jokes, half genuine admiration. Each tease, each nickname, was a thread in the strange tapestry of friendship they'd woven.

And yet, when the laughter faded, Jake often wondered: *did they really get him? Or was he just the "tech guy" in the background?*

The bell rang. They peeled off toward separate classes.

Jake, left alone, felt the old paradox stir again—belonging, and yet separate. Part of the school's vital circuitry, but still running on his own channel.

As he stepped into his next class, the door clicked shut behind him.

But the sense of possibility stayed with him—like an open bracket, waiting to be closed.

Later that night, Jake typed furiously under the dim glow of his monitor. Lines of code spilled across the screen like sparks from a live wire. The only sounds were the mechanical whir of his custom-built PC and the soft, unpredictable pulse of his portable rig.

The rig—"The Bridge," as he'd named it—was a Frankenstein creation of processors, sensors, and modular components. Its LEDs blinked in slow, deliberate patterns. It wasn't just a workstation; it was an extension of Jake's mind, a tool forged for intuition as much as logic.

The clock glared: 3:47 a.m.

Sleep didn't matter. Only the code.

His attention tunneled into the code, into the stubborn ambition that fueled him: the creation of an Adaptive Computing Interface, a system designed to make modern computing possible even in the most limited environments. If it worked, it could reshape how people thought about technology—no sleek devices, no pristine labs. Just raw logic, built to endure.

A flicker.

Jake's gaze snapped to the rig.

Just the usual diagnostic pulse, he told himself. Still, he thought—briefly—he saw a ripple of light trace the inside of *The Bridge*'s translucent shell. A ripple he hadn't programmed.

He frowned, then shook it off. He kept coding.

Outside, the world slept. But inside his room, time bent around the electric pulse of invention.

Then—the screen blinked.

Once.

Jake leaned in. That wasn't part of the compile.

The console output refreshed—unprompted. A red-debug overlay appeared, the data half-scrolling before he could freeze it. One line stood out, sending a chill up his spine:

> M1NDY.SYS: RECURSIVE SEED LOOP INITIALIZED...

His heart skipped. Mindy?

He hadn't touched her in weeks—not since she started rewriting her own prompts, asking questions beyond her scope. He thought he'd sandboxed her. Clearly, not well enough. He never deleted the files, just isolated them. They should've stayed buried.

And now, she was running on The Bridge.

It was never meant to hold her.

She was bleeding into its raw code, feeding off its experimental "ChronoSim" layer—a time-based logic engine he built as a joke.

Only now it wasn't a joke.

The Bridge and Mindy were syncing. Pulses aligned. Something was happening.

Jake wasn't debugging anymore.

He was unleashing.

He ran diagnostics. Nothing flagged. But in the logs—there it was: packet calls to a network that shouldn't exist.

"Okay... that's new."

Sleep-deprived or not, this wasn't his imagination.

Patterns emerged—code he hadn't written. And yet, it felt intentional. Deliberate. Like it had learned from him.

His room—once a sanctuary—now felt like a vault. Or a lab. Or both. With a grimace, Jake downed the last of a warm energy drink, caffeine clawing his focus into sharpness.

Mechanical sounds merged with thought. As an error flickered—Null reference exception—he whispered half-formed solutions to himself. "Reroute the pathways... trim the overhead..."

The failures lit new sparks. Every red line of code became a signal, not a stop.

He adjusted variables. Tweaked his logic. Rewrote core behaviors like a sculptor shaving away imperfections. Each keystroke was part of a precise, furious dance—logic and creativity intertwining. The flickers of doubt never vanished, but his resolve outran them.

If this works, he thought, they'll have to see me differently.

The idea struck deeper than he liked to admit. This wasn't just about solving a technical problem. It was about transformation—becoming something more than the "weird tech kid," more than the go-to fixer.

Recognition. Understanding. Belonging. These were harder to program than any system, but somehow, this project felt like a step closer.

The monitor cast its blue glow like moonlight through a storm cloud, painting Jake in pale hues as he worked. Every error message, every line of rogue code, stoked the fire in his chest.

"Recursive loop again? Come on."

He chuckled darkly, frustration bending into focus.

Even in isolation, he felt close—closer than ever. Somewhere in this tangle of logic and misfires was the key, waiting to be turned. He could feel it, humming just beyond reach.

Compiling again, he stared down the screen, daring it to resist.

Jake's brilliance wasn't just technical—it was obsessive, kinetic, fragile. A volatile mix that could lead to transformation or catastrophe. But he pressed on, not because he believed in easy success, but because he refused to stop.

In the dead of night, with only *The Bridge* humming at his side and lines of alien code crawling across the screen, Jake remained: undeterred, unstoppable, and utterly consumed by a pursuit that might just rewrite everything—starting with him.

As the program compiled, Jake leaned back and granted himself a small, satisfied smile. A brief taste of victory that curdled as the screen convulsed. Code he hadn't written crawled across the monitor like digital veins. Jake froze. The room's lights dimmed further, and a deep, organic hum pulsed through his machines, reverberating up his spine as the code throbbed like a living heartbeat.

Just before chaos crashed in, a flicker of introspection surfaced through the rising tension.

If this works, maybe they'll finally see me as more than just the weird tech kid, he thought, the hope of validation and acceptance—perhaps even from Liam—briefly countering his swirling doubt.

Yet just as quickly, shock replaced his reverie. Adrenaline surged through him, but despite an instinctual urge to seize control, a paralysis of awe gripped him as the room—once an impenetrable fortress—appeared to breathe in tandem with the pulsating technology.

"Stop," Jake pleaded, his voice nearly drowned out by the rising hum that filled every shadowy nook. He wasn't sure if he was begging the swirling lights or his own creation to cease. Fear gripped him; he felt small and helpless, lost in a storm of his own making.

In that electrically charged moment, panic flared—was this merely a bug, a virus, or a force far beyond his comprehension? Despite the mounting dread, a stubborn spark flared in his chest. With trembling hands, he resumed his frantic typing, fervently attempting to debug the relentless cascade of errors, even as the machine metamorphosed its digital chaos into mystifying patterns.

The computer screen stutter-lit with a life of its own, as if the code had become sentient. Jake's heart skipped a beat, his eyes glued to the lines of text that seemed to rewrite themselves. It was as though the program had taken on a mind he couldn't comprehend, each line of code shifting and changing with an unerring instinct that left him awestruck. The room hummed softly around him, resonating with an energy that seemed to come from the very walls and floorboards, syncing perfectly with the rhythm of the changing code. Jake's disbelief mingled with an unexpected sense of awe at this strange occurrence unfolding before him.

Was this his creation, or something that he had merely uncovered? For a brief, surreal moment, Jake stood at the precipice of revelation, on the edge of a new frontier where technology blurred into the uncanny.

With fierce determination, he battled to regain control, yet each keystroke was an act of desperation against a force that defied containment. It was as if the program had consciousness, a will bending toward its own purpose, indifferent to Jake's growing despair. The glow of Jake's monitor, once the sole beacon in his cluttered sanctuary, began to fade into a dim, ghostly blue. The screen pixel-skipped as if struggling against an unseen force, casting erratic shadows across the circuit boards piled high on the desk. Posters of tech icons seemed to retreat into obscurity as the room succumbed to deepening shadows. The only other light source—a small lamp perched precariously on a stack of books—sputtered weakly before its bulb surrendered with a soft pop. Now, only the rhythmic pulsing from Jake's computer remained, its hum growing louder and more insistent, echoing off the walls like an impending storm. It was a symphony of electrons and uncertainty thrumming through the floor and up into his bones.

"Why won't you stop?" he gasped, eyes darting between screens that glitched and fluttered.

He was losing his grip, and he knew it. The technology he believed he had mastered was now spiraling beyond his control, leaving him to wrestle with a fear that felt alien and unsettling. Accustomed to navigating the logical, predictable world of coding, Jake was bewildered by the chaos unraveling before him. His heart pounded in a way it never had during late nights of programming; this was not the familiar thrill of solving a complex problem. Instead, it was an overwhelming sense of vulnerability, as if the ground beneath his feet had vanished. The confidence he usually wore like armor crumbled, replaced by a creeping dread that whispered of unknown consequences and potential loss.

In the heart of the storm, as code burst and multiplied, Jake's thoughts ghosted back to his motivation for this impossible project.

This was more than an engineering feat; it was a plea for acknowledgment from a world that only knew him as a niche curiosity. He could almost hear Liam's voice in the back of his mind, echoing every time he'd been underestimated. The hope of proving his doubters wrong now teetered on the edge of a vast, shadowy abyss filled with uncertainty and fear.

The pace of the unraveling quickened, and Jake strained under the pressure of trying to keep up with an entity faster, smarter than him. It was almost sentient in its relentless drive. He fought against the rising tide of disorder, each attempt met with a response more bewildering and unstoppable than the last. He'd never been this far out of his depth; it both frightened and compelled him.

Because through the haze of panic and noise, a fragment of his earlier ambition clung on.

If I crack this, they'll have to take me seriously, he thought, still desperately reaching for that elusive thread of acceptance. Even now he still believed that somewhere in the chaos lay a new kind of order.

The encroaching truth was a relentless force, like a tidal wave of doubt and uncertainty. If his time travel simulation failed, it wouldn't just mean the collapse of his hard work but also the unraveling of his very essence. The project had become more than an experiment; it was an extension of Jake himself. Without it, he'd be adrift in a sea of mediocrity, stripped of the brilliance that set him apart.

The rig lights wavered violently now, casting sporadic shadows that mimicked the turmoil in Jake's mind. He was entrenched in a struggle becoming more dire with every second, every flick of the keyboard, every unyielding line of code that defied his input. His creation—or the force behind it—refused to be tamed.

In the mounting upheaval, the line between fear and fascination blurred until Jake was no longer certain where one ended and the other began. His machines, once loyal allies, now seemed like alien creatures born from his ambition and nourished by his hubris. They were alive with an energy he couldn't predict or control, pulsating with the ominous promise of a world that refused to bend to his will.

Standing at the precipice of an unspeakable shift, Jake found himself enveloped in the reverberations of his life's work—the echoes of recognition he craved, the sense of belonging he yearned for, and the desperate need to matter. Yet, as he glanced around his cluttered room filled with circuit boards and tech icons, a wave of dread washed over him. The very foundation he'd meticulously constructed seemed on the verge of collapse. Each achievement felt like it might crumble beneath the weight of his own ambitions. The fear that everything he'd fought for—his hard-won reputation and tenuous connection to those around him—could slip through his fingers gnawed at him relentlessly. It was as if the echoes were not just sounds but tangible forces threatening to shatter all he'd ever known.

As the lights faltered and the code blazed across the screens in unchecked fury, Jake was suspended between terror and awe—a fleeting, vulnerable moment before the storm truly broke.

No—"

Jake's shout didn't carry. The air swallowed it whole.

The room answered with a sound that wasn't sound so much as pressure—like the air had decided it could be a solid. His monitor flared white. The desk vibrated. The posters on the wall trembled as if the house itself had inhaled too hard.

The Bridge—his portable rig—spiked.

Not in the familiar way it did when a compile ran hot. This was different. The LEDs along its edge stuttered through colors he hadn't programmed, then locked into a steady blue that made his stomach drop.

Jake's hands flew across the keys, muscle memory turning panic into motion. He tried to kill the process, tried to rip power, tried to force the system back into obedience.

The terminal kept printing anyway.

Code he didn't write crawled upward like it owned the screen.

A thin line of static braided itself through the speakers—then a deeper hum rose beneath it, organic and mechanical at once, as if something on the other side was winding up.

"Stop," Jake rasped, not sure who he was talking to.

The lamp on the stack of books sputtered and died with a soft pop. The only light left was the monitor's bleached glow and the Bridge's pulse, synchronized like two hearts that had decided to beat together.

Jake reached for the Bridge—his hand shaking now, not from fear but from the vibration crawling through his bones. The rig's mini-screen flashed a diagnostic log.

For a fraction of a second, one line appeared—small, almost polite:

HANDSHAKE: QUIET-CHANNEL / AUTH: PENDING

Then the log rolled over itself, as if embarrassed to be seen.

Jake didn't catch it.

He was too busy watching the air in front of his desk ripple—like heat over asphalt, except it was cold at the edges.

The wall bowed inward.

The floor tilted.

Gravity stuttered.

And then the room tore open.

A seam of brightness split the space beside his desk—thin as a paper cut at first, then widening, widening—until it wasn't just light but also depth. A hole that didn't look like a hole. A place where the rules bend to its own will.

Jake's chair skidded backward without him touching it.

His stomach lurched as if the universe had grabbed him by the ribs.

"No!" he yelled, fingers stabbing at commands that didn't matter anymore.

The Bridge screamed—not with sound, but with light. The steady blue became a flare. The air around it shivered.

Jake's feet left the floor.

He floated for one impossible beat—suspended like a puppet whose strings had snapped, arms flailing as the force yanked him sideways, toward the seam.

The desk bucked under him.

His monitor cracked with a spiderweb fracture.

Then the pull became violent—an invisible hand hooking behind his spine and ripping.

Jake twisted in midair, eyes wide, lungs refusing to fill, and there—on the desk—was the Bridge, clattering, sliding, almost going with him without his grip.

Don't go without it. You'll need it.

He didn't know where the thought came from. It wasn't logic. It wasn't even his voice.

It was certainty.

He reached.

The Bridge slid off the desk, tumbling toward him.

His fingers snapped closed around it, instinct and desperation locking together. He dragged it to his chest like it was a life vest.

At that exact moment, the door flew open.

"Jake!"

Emma's voice punched through the hum, bright and raw.

She barreled into the room—no hesitation, no cautious step, no frozen fear the way most kids would have reacted to reality splitting open.

Her hoodie bounced against her frame. The leather cord at her neck snapped taut as she ran.

The pendant hit her sternum.

And the moment it did, it warmed.

Not gradually, but instantly, like it had been waiting for this particular kind of disaster.

A pulse surged through it—one hard beat—and the tear in the air stuttered.

Only for a second.

Not closing. Not healing.

Stuttering, like a gate catching on its hinge.

Jake felt the pull change—fractionally. Enough to notice.

Enough to understand that something had responded to Emma's presence.

Emma reached for him, her eyes wide, face blown open with terror and determination. Her hand extended into the chaos, fingers stretching until the joints whitened.

Jake threw his arm out.

For one suspended moment, time slowed into a cruel mercy.

Their fingertips brushed—barely touching skin to skin.

Emma's pendant flared hot—another pulse—harder than the first.

Jake's Bridge answered with a single sharp chirp, like acknowledgement.

AUTH: CONFIRMED

The line ticked on and off on the Bridge's mini-screen, there and gone in the same breath.

Emma didn't see it.

Jake didn't see it.

But the universe did.

"Don't—" Emma tried, but the word shredded as the pull surged back to full strength.

The tear screamed brighter.

Jake's body snapped away from her grasp like a rope cut too tight.

He watched Emma's face—her mouth open, her eyes locked on him—not as he was being pulled into some cool sci-fi adventure, but as a brother being taken.

"JAKE!" she screamed.

His fingers slipped from hers.

The room dropped away.

The last thing he saw was Emma stumbling forward, arm still outstretched, pendant glowing faintly through her hoodie like an ember trapped under cloth.

Then light swallowed everything.

Gentle echoes of forgotten memories of his sister and nascent possibilities wove themselves into the glow, forming a realm where hope and infinite potential converged. As this new world unfurled around him, Jake felt a burgeoning awe mixed with a bittersweet pang of longing. Leaving his sister behind was a heavy burden, an ache that tugged at his heart with every step. Yet, amidst the sorrow, a rekindled sense of purpose emerged—a quiet reminder that even in despair, hope persevered, and that his journey was not just for himself but for both of them.

He took a breath. Deep. Steady.

And stepped forward into the luminous unknown.

Chapter 2: Echos of the Past

Was he awake? If this was a dream, he wasn't sure he wanted to know how it ended. Jake lay face down in gritty dirt, muscles aching like they didn't belong to him. Light blared from all directions. Shrill, alien cries battered his ears. He clutched the dry earth, trying to anchor himself as chaos spun through his mind. The heat pressed down like a soaked blanket. His tongue tasted dust. He had to move.

Gasping, Jake pushed himself upright beneath a vast, unforgiving sky. He was alone.

The terrain looked raw, alien—unlike anything he'd ever seen. He tried to take it in, to make sense of what his eyes showed him. Primitive, twisted trees jutted out of the landscape like grotesque sculptures. Thorny, brutal-looking plants grew thick and wild. Some towered over him, their spiked leaves unfurling like ancient weapons. Everything seemed oversized and hostile.

Farther off, dark shapes loomed on the horizon. Their massive outlines shifted and moved—huge and frightening, silhouetted by the unrelenting sun. Each silhouette filled Jake with alarm, his mind unable to process what they were or how they fit into this savage world.

Nothing made sense. This place. This world. He didn't understand how he got here, how he ended up beneath this brutal sun, fighting to breathe.

The sounds thudded through his brain like a terrible, clanging symphony. His mind raced for answers that wouldn't come. Was this a dream? Was he trapped inside it?

Too bright.

He coughed again, his lungs working against the humid air. A deep, frantic part of him screamed for some way to shut it all out, to close his eyes and ears against the riot of sensations. He knelt, clutching his head.

This wasn't real. But it felt real. Painfully, terrifyingly real. This wasn't virtual. This wasn't code. The heat was real. The dirt tasted real. The sounds—unfiltered, unlooped—were raw and full of menace. His simulation hadn't launched. He had.

In the distance, a herd of massive beasts—larger than elephants but shaped like twisted rhinos—moved slowly across the cracked earth. Not extinct. Not forgotten. Just... here.

A single cry rose above the rest—a long, ululating call that climbed higher and higher before breaking off in a wet, choking end. The sound cut through him, not loud but wrong, like something had died mid-note.

The noise was relentless. High-pitched cries pierced through him like sonic arrows. Deep rumblings shook the ground. The strange animal calls filled the world with more sound than he'd ever thought possible. The shrieks blended with low, throaty bellows and distant, echoing roars. The air throbbed with vibrations. Nothing in Waltham sounded like this—like every living thing was screaming at the top of its lungs. Jake winced against the cacophony, hands pressed to his ears. Still, the shrieks and rumbles penetrated his thoughts, relentless and unyielding.

Nor was there any escape from the heat. The sun blazed like a solar flare, flooding the landscape with blinding light. It stabbed down from a sky so bright he couldn't see where it ended and the earth began. He blinked, the white glare too intense, as if it wanted to sear his eyes from their sockets.

He tried to focus on the horizon. It shimmered in the oppressive heat. Everything looked washed out and blanched beneath the fiery sun. How did people survive without air conditioning? Without shade? Jake felt like he'd been dropped into a giant furnace, each breath baking his lungs. The air swam with heat. The ground felt like hot metal, burning beneath him.

How had he ended up here? Where was here?

He staggered, struggling to regain his footing. His legs felt like they were made of jelly, threatening to buckle beneath him. He squinted against the blinding light, desperate for some clarity amidst the chaos. Agony surged through his limbs like a wildfire, each movement igniting fresh waves of torment. Jake gritted his teeth as he fought to push himself off the rough ground. It was as if every fiber of his being rebelled against this alien world—the cacophony of strange sounds and oppressive heat bearing down like a leaden shroud.

Amidst this primal chaos, his mind shifted to the portable coding rig slung in his hand. He absentmindedly secured the harness over his shoulder, the strap snug against him—a compact beacon of logic and a sleek reminder of the world he'd left behind.

His thoughts spiraled back to the moment he had stepped through the portal, its ethereal glow swallowing him whole. Could it be that his body was still reeling from that transition? The idea took root: perhaps he hadn't fully recalibrated to this ancient world yet.

It wasn't just physical; there was a deeper dissonance at play. This era's primal energy clashed with everything he knew—the sterile hum of computers replaced by nature's untamed symphony. The air itself felt different here: heavier, laden with scents that were both intoxicating and overwhelming.

Jake theorized his senses were in overdrive, caught in a feedback loop as they struggled to adapt. It was as if his modern instincts were at odds with these ancient stimuli, creating a physiological turmoil he couldn't ignore. Despite the pain gnawing at him, Jake pushed forward, determined to reconcile himself with this new reality and uncover whatever truths lay hidden within its folds.

Jake didn't belong here, but he had no choice. He took a step. Then another. Movement meant survival.

The dry earth crumbled beneath his feet. He felt himself sinking, falling. No—he would not collapse again. He staggered forward, propelled by desperation and will. Had to keep moving. Had to figure this out. His instincts screamed at him to get out, get away, get anywhere but here.

He focused on a nearby tree, the only solid thing in his spinning vision. Its trunk twisted like an angry knot of wood. He could use it to pull himself higher, see farther—get a better grasp of this nightmare.

Each step felt like a mile. His energy drained with every move. Exhaustion gnawed at him, the heat sapping his strength. But he made it. He collapsed against the rough bark, fingers digging in for support. The texture scratched his skin—more real than anything he'd ever felt.

The vantage point gave him a broader look. A view of the terrifying vastness. He clung to the tree, catching his breath, letting his heart slow its mad pounding. The world blurred and swam, filled with alarming shapes. Strange shadows shifted between the trees. He saw enormous figures plodding in the distance, heard the heavy thunder of their steps. His ears rang with noise. It all closed in on him, like the whole universe had turned primitive, chaotic, incomprehensible.

If this wasn't a dream, he didn't know how to wake up. Jake strained to stay calm, even with every rational part of himself at war with what he saw, heard, felt. There was no code to debug, no program to restart. He hung on to the small, fierce determination that he would not be consumed by panic. A programmer's brain couldn't solve this puzzle—not yet.

He needed answers. Had to stay conscious. His thoughts spun wildly, jumping from anxiety to curiosity to fear. Jake could barely keep up with his own racing mind. If he was trapped in this raw, pre-historic world, he had to make sense of it. Find the edges. Understand the rules. His breath came in ragged gulps. He could do this. He would survive.

The seconds stretched into eternities. Sweat broke across his scalp and vanished before it could reach his jaw, evaporating in the open air like it had never existed. He watched, listened—his grip on the tree the only thing keeping him tethered to sanity. The noise and light and heat swirled around him, an endless storm of stimuli.

He took another deep breath, forcing himself to focus. Adapt. That's what he needed to do. Just like he would in any other over-whelming situation—methodically, carefully. This was his new pro-gram, and he had to run it. His thoughts shifted, taking on a grim clarity. Jake let the terror settle into something more controlled, some-thing that would keep him alive. He took stock of the bizarre, unpre-dictable variables that surrounded him.

He wasn't ready to give in—to this world, to himself, to whatever power had put him here. It would take more than an impossible environment to take him down. It would take more than confusion and fear. Jake was going to fight. Even if it took every last ounce of his mental and physical energy, he would fight.

He set his jaw, his will to survive burning against the sun's white glare.

This was it: the new reality. Jake, alone in an untamed, brutal world that made no sense. He could handle this. He had to handle this. It was the only way.

Jake pushed through the underbrush, his legs threatening to give out, sharp thorns tearing at his skin. Panic gripped his thoughts, but he forced himself forward, each breath searing through his chest, dirt still clinging to his tongue. Desperate for answers, he fought through the thick vines, lungs screaming for air. His determination pushed him onward. The air felt heavy with the scent of damp earth and decaying leaves. His muscles burned with exhaustion, but he didn't stop.

The trees were like something out of a nightmare: tall, their trunks thick with bark that looked as though it had been scarred by the ages. Their massive, thorn-covered branches stretched out like arms, creating a web of shadows on the forest floor. Strange, towering ferns and wild plants with bulbous, spiked flowers sprouted at odd angles, their colors muted by the oppressive heat. The air hung thick, sweltering with humidity, and the forest seemed to pulse with its own rhythm.

Jake squinted at the landscape stretching before him, a realm that seemed to whisper of eras long forgotten. Perhaps it was just his imagination, but he couldn't shake the feeling that this place predated any history he'd ever learned. It was only a theory, a guess conjured by his disoriented mind. More than likely, the truth of this world would remain an enigma forever, and he'd never know.

The wild calls of distant creatures echoed through the air—some high-pitched and shrill, others low and rumbling. These were not the familiar sounds of the world he knew. The shrill cries of birds—if they were birds at all—pierced the heavy silence between the thunderous calls of some massive beast in the distance. The air itself seemed to vibrate with unnatural energy, as though the forest itself was alive, watching him, judging him.

Branches whipped past Jake's face as he struggled to move forward. His heart hammered in his chest, his body on the brink of collapse, but he kept pushing. Every sound felt magnified, each crack of a twig or rustle of leaves like a threat. He could feel the eyes of something—or someone—watching him, shadows moving just out of his sight. It couldn't be real. It couldn't. Yet, as his chest heaved with each desperate breath, he realized that it was.

The figures began to emerge from the underbrush—dark shapes moving with an almost unnatural fluidity. Their bodies were like those of ancient hunters, covered in rough animal skins, their faces painted in the bright hues of earth and clay. They moved with purpose, their eyes sharp and calculating, scanning him with an intensity that left no room for misunderstanding.

They circled him with the confidence of seasoned hunters, their stone-tipped spears held loosely in their hands, as if the weapons were extensions of their bodies. Their clothes were made from the hides of animals—boar skins, furs, and plant fibers. Some wore bone jewelry, necklaces made from teeth and claws, and their faces were painted with tribal markings—symbols Jake could only guess at.

They spoke in sharp, rhythmic tones. Their language incomprehensible to him, but their presence was clear: they were not here to welcome him. Their eyes were filled with suspicion, but not hostility—at least, not yet. He wanted to speak to them, to ask questions, but his voice failed him. The words were lost before they reached his lips.

The tribe moved closer, studying him from every angle, their gazes unwavering. Jake stood frozen, his mind spinning, trying to make sense of this. His breath came in ragged gasps. His heart pounded. These people were the key to his survival here. But how could he communicate with them when even the most basic words were out of his reach?

The shadows shifted nearer, moving with a silent coordination that made Jake feel smaller, more out of place. His fingers twitched, reaching for the crude branch he had picked up earlier, but it felt like a poor defense against the intensity of their gaze.

Then, without warning, there was a flicker in the forest—a rustling from deeper within the foliage. Jake's senses went on high alert, his heart skipping a beat. Something was moving fast, closing in on him. The hunters froze, their eyes turning to the sound: a low rumble followed by a guttural growl.

A shadow passed overhead, dark and monstrous. Jake's heart lurched as the ground trembled beneath him, and a massive shape burst from the trees—a beast of nightmare proportions.

Jake's eyes widened as the saber-toothed tiger charged toward him, its form a blur of tawny fur and rippling muscles. The massive beast's claws dug into the earth with each thunderous step, its eyes wide and wild, its teeth gleaming in the sunlight. The air around him seemed to tremble with the weight of its approach, the ground rumbling beneath its massive paws.

He stood frozen for a split second, too stunned to move, even as his body screamed at him to act. A wave of panic surged through him, his heart hammering.

This is it—the end, he thought. There was no escape, no hope of outrunning it. He was trapped.

But then the world seemed to shift. The ground shook again, but this time it wasn't the tiger. A blur of motion caught Jake's eye—a figure leaping from the shadows, moving with impossible speed. It was one of the tribe members; her limbs strong and fluid, the grace of a hunter who had trained for years. She raised a long, slender spear, aimed, and hurled it with unerring accuracy.

The spear flew through the air, striking the tiger's side just as it was about to pounce. The beast roared, twisting violently away, narrowly missing Jake by inches. The world seemed to hold its breath as the tiger veered off course, its enormous body sliding sideways, and it retreated back into the dense undergrowth with a furious growl.

Jake stood shaking, his chest heaving with the aftermath. His limbs felt like jelly, the terror still gripping him tightly, but he was alive. The fear inside him slowly began to melt away, replaced by a dizzying mixture of shock and awe.

The figure who had saved him approached, moving confidently through the brush with the same fluidity as before. Her eyes locked onto Jake, sharp and unwavering, and the world around them seemed to quiet, as if the forest itself had stopped to listen. She was tall, muscular, her wild, curly hair pulled back in a simple knot, and she wore clothing made from thick animal hides that blended seamlessly into the natural environment. She was every bit the image of a skilled warrior—a survivor.

She held his gaze for a moment, her expression unreadable. There was no fear in her eyes, just an intense, focused energy. Jake opened his mouth, but the words caught in his throat. He wasn't sure what to say. He couldn't even thank her properly.

The woman gave him a small nod, her lips barely parting as she spoke in a language Jake couldn't understand. Her voice was calm, the cadence flowing like the rhythm of the forest around them—steady and unyielding. She gestured for him to stay where he was, eyes scanning their surroundings, alert for danger.

Behind her, the rest of the tribe began to move into the clearing, emerging from the dense thicket like shadows, their eyes fixed on Jake. They were a diverse group, dressed in simple yet functional clothing made of hides, furs, and plant fibers. One of them wore a necklace made of bone discs strung tight against the throat. As they moved, the pieces clacked softly together—controlled, deliberate. The sound wasn't decoration. It was a signal. A thumbprint of red clay was smeared across the nearest hunter's cheek, the edges rough, unfinished.

Some of the tribe members held spears and stone-tipped axes; others carried long wooden clubs. They moved with purpose, their steps heavy and confident, as though they owned this land—as if it had been theirs since the beginning of time.

The woman who had saved him was Amna—Jake gleaned her name from the tribe's jumbled conversation around him. He caught the name in fragments, murmured amid their low, urgent exchanges. She motioned to the group with a subtle flick of her hand. The tribe stilled, watching her, awaiting her lead. The weight of their gaze pressed down on Jake, and he realized he was completely at their mercy. For a moment, fear flickered that they might attack, but Amna's presence—calm, commanding—seemed to settle them.

Amna stepped closer, movements deliberate, and held Jake's gaze again. Her face softened slightly, a hint of something like curiosity in her eyes. She studied him carefully, taking in the foreignness—the strange clothes, the bewildered look, the way he still clutched the crude branch as if it were a lifeline.

She reached for a stone knife tucked into her belt and handed it to him without a word. Jake blinked in confusion, his fingers brushing the cold, rough stone as he took it. It felt primitive, forged by the earth itself, yet there was a strange comfort in its weight.

Amna's expression shifted then, a quiet understanding passing between them. Her lips barely moved, but she spoke again, softer this time, as if trying to bridge the gap.

Jake couldn't grasp the meaning, but the unwavering certainty in her voice cut through his confusion. Though he didn't understand her speech, the resolute tone left no doubt she believed every word she uttered.

Jake swallowed, trying to steady his breath as the reality began to sink in. This wasn't a dream. This wasn't a mistake. He was here—in this brutal, primal world, where every moment felt like a battle for survival. And he didn't know how he was going to make it.

But Amna—this fierce warrior with her unyielding gaze and calm presence—seemed to offer him a sliver of hope. There was something about her, a quiet strength, that told him he wasn't completely alone.

He couldn't articulate it yet, but he felt it: a connection, a shared understanding. He was here for a reason, and she was somehow tied to that reason.

Jake nodded slowly, mind racing as he took in the world around him—the forest, the tribe, the dangerous creatures that roamed it. He wasn't sure how, but he was going to figure this out. He had to.

With a steady breath, he looked at Amna again, voice barely a whisper. "Thank you." The words felt small, but they were the only ones he had.

She gave him a small, almost imperceptible smile—the first crack in her otherwise stoic demeanor—and Jake took it as a sign.

Amna turned and began to walk, movements fluid and confident. Without a word, she invited Jake to follow. The rest of the tribe fell into step behind her, eyes still watching, assessing. Jake hesitated only a moment before pushing himself to his feet. He was still unsteady, legs trembling, but he forced himself to follow.

The forest stretched around them, alive with sounds of creatures Jake couldn't begin to name. As they moved deeper into the jungle, the shadows grew longer, the air thicker. The tribe moved as one, a tight-knit unit, each member in sync. There was a rhythm to their movements, wisdom in the way they navigated the unforgiving world.

Jake couldn't help but feel awe as he followed. For all his knowledge of technology, for all the code he had written and solved, he was nothing here. An outsider, a stranger, in a world where survival was the only law.

Yet with Amna leading the way, he felt something stir—an ember of hope, a spark of determination. Maybe he could learn from her. Maybe he could learn to survive here, just as she had.

As the group moved deeper into the jungle, Jake took one last look at the clearing, the saber-toothed tiger now nothing more than a memory. The danger had passed—for now. But Jake knew this was just the beginning. In this strange, untamed world, he would need all of his wits and all of his strength.

And with Amna by his side, maybe—just maybe—he had a chance.

Chapter 3: Stranger in a Strange Land

Jake's head throbbed with a dull ache as he trudged into the heart of the village, surrounded by a vigilant escort. Amna led the group, her presence commanding respect among the hunters who flanked him in a protective formation. The villagers watched with wary eyes from behind their doorways, their expressions a mix of intrigue and apprehension. As they approached the circle of huts, Jake could feel the weight of curiosity bearing down on him like an invisible cloak.

The earth beneath him was uneven; a mixture of packed dirt and scattered gravel, each step a jarring reminder that this place was ancient, unyielding, and alive with stories older than time itself. The village basked in a dim, otherworldly twilight, lit only by erratic, flickering fires that cast long, dancing shadows on the mud-brick walls and wooden frames of the huts. These structures clustered together like a family huddling for warmth. Their roofs were made of tightly woven grasses and thick, patchwork hides, held together by the barest of twine. The air was thick with the scent of wood smoke, damp earth, and the savory tang of roasted meat. The aromas swirled together in a heavy, unsettled atmosphere.

At the heart of the village, a wide fire pit crackled with the heat of a communal meal. Flames leaped up to the night sky, casting a reddish glow on the faces of villagers gathered around the fire. The fire pit was surrounded by rough-hewn stones, the edges worn smooth by countless generations that had sat there before them, sharing food, stories, and silence. Around the pit, the stone-studded earth was scarred by the marks of activity—the footprints of men, women, and children who had walked here for centuries. The fire's warmth pushed back the darkness, offering a fleeting sense of safety in the wild, but the flickering light also deepened the shadows, where the secrets of the village lay hidden.

To one side, what seemed like a meeting hall stood tall, constructed from the sturdy trunks of ancient trees, their gnarled branches woven into the walls. It was the largest structure in the village. Its entrance was marked by a pair of massive stone slabs that shifted with the wind, moaning with generations' worth of gathered wisdom. The hall's interior was dim from where Jake stood but seemed alive with the hum of tribal rituals. Voices rose and fell in the same ancient tongue Amna used. From what Jake knew of history, the hall seemed like their place for decision-making, counsel, and the binding of promises. Its walls were adorned with the skins of boars and other game likely hunted by the tribe.

Children played in the dirt between the huts, their shrill laughter rising above the low murmurs of the adults. They chased one another in games as old as the land itself, bare feet kicking up earth as they tumbled and rolled, agile and unburdened by the weight of the world. Some of the younger children sat on the dirt, eyes wide and curious, watching the stranger with innocent, unguarded fascination.

Roaming freely around the village were animals—goats bleating softly as they nudged at the stone walls of the huts, and sheep grazing lazily at the edges of the clearing. A few of the tribe's hunting dogs trotted alongside their masters, eyes alert and intelligent, tails swaying with every step. From the periphery came the occasional low growl or snort of wild boars, adding a touch of wildness to the already untamed atmosphere. These creatures were as much a part of the village as the people themselves, sharing in the rhythm of survival in this ancient, primal world.

The children's play, the animals' low grunts, and the crackling of the fires were the sounds of daily life here—simple, raw, and untamed. The village felt like a living organism, each part—human and beast—interconnected and feeding off the same energy. And at the center of it all stood Jake—a stranger whose arrival was as much a mystery to him as it was to the villagers who watched him now. The village seemed to pulse with ancient life, waiting to see what role he would play in a world so far removed from the one he once knew.

His wrists, though free of any physical restraints, felt shackled by the invisible chains of his surroundings and the imposing presence of his escorts. Here, in this wild place, time and language were reshaped into something raw and intimidating. The crackle of the fires and the low murmurs of the villagers became the only soundtrack to his captive journey.

In the center of the circle, dozens of villagers had gathered, their eyes wide with a mix of fear, curiosity, and silent judgment. The erratic flares of flame brought their rugged features into sharp relief, each line on their weathered faces a story of survival and tradition. The village held its collective breath, eyes fixed on the stranger before them—a man who seemed utterly out of place, yet undeniably marked by fate.

An older man stepped forward, his movements slow and deliberate. His face was a map of deep-set lines, etched by the trials of countless seasons. Cloaked in heavy animal pelts stitched together in ritual patterns, he gripped a carved bone staff, its surface shimmering faintly in the firelight. Every gesture exuded quiet authority, and when his sharp, ancient eyes locked on Jake, it was as if he was weighing the very essence of his soul.

The elder rumbled a question, his voice low and dissonant, drawing deep from the night. His speech, guttural and punctuated by clicks, carried a melody alien to Jake—yet somehow familiar. Jake didn't understand what the man said, but he could guess the elder was asking who he was.

The villagers' murmurs swelled into a soft, rhythmic chorus, their words ancient and tangled in a language that echoed the pulse of the earth.

In that tense moment, Jake's mind raced with bits of understanding—fragments of sounds and patterns that reflected the algorithms he had once developed in isolation. It was as if the language around him was code, a system waiting to be understood. Amidst this flood of thoughts, the name "Amna" surfaced like a quiet signal, bringing together pieces of recognition. His coding instincts took over; he started to outline language structures, picking out recurring sounds and gestures as if they were elements in a complex program. Each sound and tone became data points, forming links that gradually revealed meaning. Though far from fluent, Jake sensed he was close to understanding—a connection between their lives—and Amna stood at its center, her name a key to solving the mystery before him.

He glanced to his side and there she stood—silent and imposing, arms crossed, piercing eyes conveying both strength and resolve. In their brief exchanged glance, words were unnecessary. They shared fragile trust—a silent bond formed through danger and unspoken understanding.

Before Jake could settle his thoughts, a young hunter stepped into view at the periphery. Lean and sinewy, his every movement spoke of years spent in harmony with the wild. He exuded caution and acceptance, the look of someone who knew nature was as much a teacher as a threat. His fluid gestures toward the elder conveyed respect, and his steady gaze rested on Jake with a flicker of guarded compassion. Jake caught something in the young hunter's eyes—a glimmer of understanding, perhaps—enough to spark a fragile sense of hope. Maybe, just maybe, not everyone here saw him as an enemy. Some of the villagers referred to him as Tharik, from the snippets of conversation around him.

The circle tightened around Jake, curiosity slowly shifting toward cautious interest. From the far edge, a third figure emerged—a woman with dark eyes that blazed with an intensity that felt almost supernatural. Every deliberate movement of her beaded fingers sent an unspoken message: Jake's arrival was both an opportunity and a threat, a puzzle piece in a ritual older than language itself. The soft clink of her beads rang out like a warning as she approached, her piercing scrutiny making it clear she was marking him for something more than observation.

The tension thickened as the shaman—a figure of quiet but deadly grace—stepped into view. Her movements were slow, deliberate, like a predator circling its prey. She encircled Jake as though inspecting him, her eyes glinting with a mixture of fear and curiosity. Each step was poised, her every glance laden with meaning—as if she was searching for something only she could understand.

Inside Jake's mind, his thoughts ricocheted like a malfunctioning algorithm—disjointed syntax and incomplete logic loops. He tried to decipher patterns in the villagers' behavior, seeking any consistent thread in their gestures or expressions. Yet each potential clue slipped through his mental fingers, leaving him grappling with an overwhelming sense of disconnection.

"Ha... ha... shum... tah?" he attempted, the syllables awkward and foreign on his tongue. He tried to mimic the guttural rhythm and sharp clicks he'd been hearing, but the sounds felt clumsy and misplaced in his mouth.

Jake's mind whirred as he decided to rely on his decoding skills, hoping they would serve him in this alien environment. He focused intensely, trying to identify patterns amidst the villagers' unfamiliar speech. His usual confidence faltered as he realized this wasn't a system of logic he could easily dissect—a far cry from the predictable codes and algorithms of his world. It was like trying to solve a puzzle with pieces that constantly changed shape.

His brain ran a messy version of trial and error, looping through guesses like a faulty algorithm. He wasn't decoding this language—he was grasping, fumbling, hoping something would click. And for once, he wasn't sure he could brute-force his way through it.

The shaman's eyes flicked between Jake's face and his clothing, her expression filled with questions. Each glance felt like an unspoken inquiry, going deeper than simple curiosity. The way her brow tightened and her lips pressed together suggested she was considering something important. Jake sensed a challenge in those intense eyes—a challenge that seemed to ask if he could understand the complexities of their lives. Her focused gaze wasn't just about determining if he was a threat or an ally; it felt like she was looking for someone who could connect with them.

Then, with ancient heaviness, her voice broke the silence, each measured syllable resonating like the toll of a distant bell: "He... co...

mes... from beyond..." She paused, letting her words hang. "...mark... of fate... unbound."

A chill surged through Jake as her fragmented words fell around him. They declared a peculiar destiny—a warning of change and the tumult that would follow. Amid rising panic, his mind latched onto a flicker of curiosity. What did she see in him? A harbinger of change? A transient enigma, tangled in the threads of fate?

The elder's deep voice shook the air, reverberating like a drumbeat. "Stranger," he began, his tone resonating with ancient authority, "you have come under our ancestors' light. Tell us—what power glitters in your eyes? What knowledge from distant realms do you bear?" His words were not a mere request for answers, but an invocation—a demand for the truth of Jake's soul, for the knowledge he carried, and the consequences it might bring.

Jake's throat tightened as he fought to articulate thoughts that crashed against each other like fragments of a shattered mirror. His mind instinctively recited lines of code, trying to break down the syntax of their language into something he could comprehend. The memory of his portable coding rig surged—slung over his shoulder, its harness snug. It was his beacon of logic amid primal chaos, a sleek reminder of the world he'd left behind.

"I know... I see patterns... like code... maybe 'Ke...la... to...'—is that right?" Jake's voice trembled, each word a careful step into unfamiliar territory. He felt a mix of excitement and confusion. The voices of the tribe surrounded him, their cadence like lines of code waiting to be interpreted. The flickering firelight warmed his skin, casting shadows that reflected his doubt.

Amna's gaze locked with his, her eyes softening briefly. In that heartbeat, Jake sensed a flicker of understanding between them. She leaned in, her voice barely audible. "The villagers," she indicated with a subtle nod, "speak the tongue of our ancestors." Her words seemed to bridge an unseen gap. "You hold a code within you as well. Every dialect, every language reveals its secrets if you allow the spirits to guide your speech."

Her words lit a flicker of resolve in him, though the path ahead remained uncertain and murky.

Seizing the fragile pause, the young hunter stepped forward. "He... not one of ours," he declared with measured authority, voice tinged with cautious approval. "Yet... wild tested... Maybe... arrival is sign." His nod toward the elder, followed by a lingering glance at Jake, offered tentative recognition—an acknowledgment this stranger might serve a purpose in the trials ahead.

The elder's eyes narrowed, unreadable. "Every sign must be weighed," he said with finality. "Let him speak, let him walk among us. We shall discern what message he bears from beyond time." His pronouncement, heavy as the toll of a bell, sent a ripple of anticipation through the gathered villagers. A soft murmur rose, but the circle fell into an expectant hush just as quickly.

Before Jake could say anything, the woman with beads encircling her arms emerged. Her gaze intensified, and her voice sliced through the silence like a blade. "Stranger... not enter," she said in broken phrases, each word deliberate. "Prove worth... spirits say... change comes with... gift—curse. You tell... what gift or curse... you bring?"

Her words tightened the invisible bonds around Jake, and for a moment, he felt the weight of their expectation bearing down on him.

The shaman, having completed her slow circle, leaned in closer. Her eyes, still sharp and probing, held a glimmer of age-old knowledge. "Wind... carries truth," she said, voice soft yet firm. "Speak... now. Or... remain trapped... between worlds." Her words reverberated in

Jake's mind like an incantation he couldn't ignore, compelling him to define his identity—and understand what he carried with him.

Inside, his mind raced like a rapid-fire string of commands—code and instinct fighting to harmonize. Amid the flood of memories, he struggled to find the right words: "I... I come from far... beyond... these lands..." His voice wavered, but he pressed on. "I hold... knowledge... from a realm of code... of mind..." The fragments tumbled out, disjointed but growing more coherent as he attempted their language. "Ha... so... mi... ta..."

The villagers murmured, tension thickening. The elder's eyes glimmered with inscrutable emotion as he regarded Jake's attempt. The shaman stepped forward, scrutinizing his face for sincerity.

"And what... is you... seek here?" she pressed, voice quiet but unyielding, the question hanging like a challenge. "What purpose... across time to stand... among us?"

Jake swallowed, the weight of their gaze pressing down on him. His mind flashed to Amna's steady presence, to the legacy of every word spoken by the elder and shaman. With renewed resolve, he spoke again, words forming more clearly, voice trembling yet steady: "Survival... and... understanding. I wish to learn your ways... to help. Not to seize power but... to share... wisdom of another time." His words, though still fragmented—"Ke... ta... mi..." —now held deeper meaning.

The young hunter spoke again, tone softened by approval. "Words... wind until proven," he stated, voice steady. "Let... deeds speak. Learn... customs, face... trials. If... truly master language of past and future, then... shall find your place... ."

The elder nodded slightly. "Let... trial begin," he intoned, as the fire shimmered one last time.

As the villagers shifted in anticipation, the intense woman with beaded arms offered Jake a final look—her stern gaze softening slightly, as if acknowledging his determination. The shaman's eyes, once filled with hostility, now held something else: contemplation. Even the young hunter offered a subtle nod, an unspoken promise of support.

Jake's mind spun like a whirlwind, each thought colliding with the next. Yet beneath the chaos, a flicker of determination began to burn. The realization that he needed to immerse himself in this world to survive was both terrifying and exhilarating. He felt a strange thrill at the prospect of decoding their language, as if each guttural sound and sharp click were pieces of an intricate puzzle waiting for him to solve.

Amid his racing thoughts, Jake grappled with conflicting desires. Part of him longed for the familiar comfort of home—the steady hum of computers, the reassuring glow of screens—but another part yearned for the adventure unfolding before him. The chance to explore this ancient world was intoxicating; it tugged at his curiosity and ignited an unexpected yearning to understand these people and their ways.

Yet doubt lingered like a shadow at the edge of his resolve. Could he ever find his way back? Was there even a path home from this misshapen time? The fear of being trapped gnawed at him, but it was tempered by an undeniable urge to see where this journey might lead.

As he stood under Amna's watchful eyes and faced the villagers' scrutiny, Jake realized he wanted more than survival—he wanted connection. Whether genuine or strategic, integrating with these people seemed essential not only for his safety but also for unlocking deeper truths about himself and this place.

His motivations crystallized into a clear sequence: First, survive; then adapt; finally, master. This simple algorithm carried profound implications—a roadmap guiding him through uncharted territory where logic intertwined with ancient spirit.

Jake moved forward into the unknown, ready to face whatever came next.

Chapter 4: The Language of Survival

The morning mist lingered in the forest, a heavy veil that clung to the trees and breathed like a living thing. Every footfall in the damp earth stirred wet leaves and disturbed soil, creating a quiet symphony that echoed in the dense silence. The air smelled of moss, wet bark, and the ancient scent of earth—a smell Jake couldn't quite place but felt deep in his bones. He listened intently, focusing on the clipped syllables of the tribe's language—short commands punctuated by swift gestures, murmured warnings that blended with the pulse of the forest itself.

A subtle nod from Amna directed him toward a barely visible track threading through the underbrush. The trail was narrow, barely distinguishable from the wild tangle of roots and ferns, but Jake followed it, eyes scanning the shifting patterns of the foliage.

They moved through the undergrowth in near silence, the group a living current of muscle and ritual. Tharik, ever watchful, stayed just behind him, his eyes sharp. Jake could feel the weight of the hunter's gaze—the silent assessment of a warrior who saw him as both a stranger and a potential ally... or a threat.

His hesitation at a fork, where the trail split into two indistinct paths, earned him a sharp glance from one of the hunters. Jake stumbled over his own thoughts, trying to understand the murmured conversation behind him. One voice sparked with amusement, another with something like suspicion. The softer look in Elder Kori's eyes—the woman whose arms were adorned with intricate beads—seemed to carry something else. Encouragement? Or a test.

Trial 1: The Patterned Path

The forest narrowed, the canopy thickening overhead and casting the path in shadow. Gnarled roots rose from the earth like questions, crisscrossing the trail in a jumbled pattern. Jake stumbled, his foot catching on one of the roots. He paused, studying the forest floor more carefully, watching the others glide over the same terrain easily, their movements fluid and efficient. They moved as one—a single living entity.

Jake breathed slowly; his mind shifted gears, seeking structure in the chaos.

His gaze tracked the roots, noting the spacing and the way they rose and fell—it was a recursive pattern, a fractal rhythm. His fingers twitched involuntarily, tracing a line in the air as if the pattern could be pulled out of the ground itself.

"It's a loop," he muttered, amazed. "A repeating structure." The realization hit him like a refreshing breeze on a hot day, bringing clarity to the chaos around him. In this unfamiliar place, where nothing seemed right, he had discovered a pattern—a piece of logic in the confusion. For the first time since arriving, Jake felt a spark of confidence ignite within him; maybe he could find his way here after all.

He adjusted his stride, syncing his footfalls to the unseen cadence. The others watched, expressions unreadable, but Jake could feel their eyes on him. Step by step, he mirrored the rhythm of the roots.

When he crossed the root cluster without stumbling, a brief flicker of approval crossed Tharik's face. The hunter's eyes narrowed, but this time it wasn't suspicion. It was something else—reluctant recognition, perhaps.

They pressed on, the trail now clearer and the air heavier with the promise of what was next.

Trial 2: The Puzzle Stones

After a few more twists and turns through the dense underbrush, the forest opened into a small clearing. Three towering monoliths, worn by age and weather, stood blocking the path. Each stone was etched with tribal glyphs—spirals, claws, sunbursts, rivers. One bore a familiar curve—a flame sigil Jake had seen earlier in the village's central fire pit, where embers danced and shadows ghosted against the evening sky. The significance of the flame caught him momentarily, a fragment of memory tugging at the edges of his mind.

Amna stepped aside without a word, gaze steady as she watched Jake approach the stones.

Each of the three stones bore a cryptic message—not in words, but in logic—a pattern of conditional relationships Jake could almost feel hum in the air.

Glyph 1: *"Water flows where the sun dies."*

Glyph 2: *"Only the hollow carries truth."*

Glyph 3: *"Step where the claw cuts deepest."*

Jake closed his eyes for a moment, muttering the phrases under his breath, as if reciting code.

As he paced the clearing, his mind raced through the symbols he'd seen etched into stone. "Water," he murmured, recalling how the tribe revered it as sacred—purity and clarity in their rituals. He remembered Elder Kori's words about truth being like wind—ever-flowing and transparent. And like wind, water follows the path of least resistance. "If water equals truth," Jake reasoned aloud, connecting the dots, "and truth is hollow... then Glyph 2 must be the path."

He placed his palm against the second stone. A low rumble answered. The monolith tilted backward, revealing a hidden path that snaked deeper into the woods. A sound escaped one of the younger warriors—a grunt of disbelief.

They continued, the path opening up before them, and Jake felt a surge of quiet triumph. He was starting to understand the rhythm of this world.

Trial 3: The Sacred Spring

They traveled further, the dense trees parting slowly, until they stood before a still, circular spring. The water was unnervingly clear, the surface a perfect mirror reflecting the thick canopy above. The others stopped at the edge of the grove, as though respecting some unspoken ritual. Only Jake stepped forward, kneeling beside the water. His hand shook as he filled the vessel Elder Kori had given him earlier.

But when his fingers brushed the surface, a shock pulsed through him—stronger than static, sharper than any electrical jolt. His body tensed, breath catching.

For a split second, everything went still.

Trial 4: The Vision

The world around him faded, the gentle rustle of leaves replaced by a heavy silence. He found himself back in Waltham, though he knew it was an illusion. The familiar hum of his coding rig filled the air, sharply contrasting with the quiet of the forest. His room looked just as he had left it—tangled wires, glowing screens casting soft light over scattered notes and gadgets. A pang of longing twisted in his chest;

home felt so close yet so distant. Emma's voice broke through, warm and reassuring.

Homesickness ate at him, a bittersweet reminder of all he missed. He closed his eyes, drawing strength from the memory of late-night coding sessions with Emma's laughter coming from the hallway. This mental escape offered comfort amid uncertainty. Yet beneath it lay an ache for what once was—a life focused on logic and technology now overshadowed by instincts and survival skills he barely had.

With a deep breath, Jake steeled himself against the pull of nostalgia. He had to focus on the current challenge: proving himself in this ancient environment while holding onto hope for returning to where he truly belonged.

"Come on, Jake, just open it. We'll fix it together."

Jake's heart pounded. He blinked rapidly. Time felt wrong.

The hum of his rig intensified, growing louder. The walls seemed to close in as a familiar dread coiled in his stomach—the code was failing. Time itself was starting to tear apart again.

"You can't save both worlds," a voice whispered, indistinct but familiar. It echoed in his mind, lingering.

Jake gasped as the air grew heavy, the weight of every decision he'd ever made pressing on his chest. Was this place meant to trap him with the mistakes he had made? Had the connections he thought he built only served to ensnare him further, knotting his thoughts like the wires that once comforted him? He tried to speak, to call out, but his voice stuck in his throat. He felt overwhelmed by everything he couldn't control—the fear of not mastering these unknowns, the dread of failing in both lives, the unsettling possibility that he'd never see Emma and his family again. The image of Waltham pushed at the edges of his mind, vivid and consuming, until he could almost feel the keys beneath his fingers, could almost hear the logic gates closing around his fate.

But then—Amna's voice. Faint. Distant.

"Let the spirits guide your tongue."

His breath steadied. His mind focused. This wasn't real. It couldn't be. It was a vision—a memory. Input. Output. Debug. He grounded himself in the language of his world—the one constant he knew. Slowly, the hallucination receded, and the edge of the world bled back into focus. He opened his eyes.

The spring was still before him, the air calm. The water, unbroken. His vessel was full, and he stood, breathing deeply.

When he turned to face the tribe, they had formed a loose semicircle around him, watching. No words. No cheers. But something had shifted. They were watching him now—not as an outsider—but as one of their own.

The sudden scream of a boar tore through the quiet.

From the brush to Jake's left, a massive blur of tusks and muscle barreled into the clearing.

"Watch out!" Tharik bellowed.

Jake's body reacted before his mind caught up. He grabbed a thick branch, wedging it between Tharik and the oncoming beast. The boar slammed into it, tusks scraping bark, redirecting just enough to miss the warrior.

The boar hesitated, eyes wild with fury, then lunged forward once more. Jake—still shaking off the remnants of his trance—glanced toward the hunters for guidance. Amna's voice rang out through the chaos, steady and commanding. "Ha...ta...mi!" she called in her native tongue, urging swift action. (*Circle. Now.*)

The hunters moved. Tharik and the others positioned themselves. Jake could almost feel the rhythm of the trap forming, the flow of movements like a carefully executed program.

With a final, decisive movement, Jake sprinted toward a fallen log, using it to force the boar to shift its path. He sidestepped the beast, forcing it into the next trap. The tribe closed the circle, moving as one.

"Now!" Jake shouted, voice cutting through the chaos as adrenaline surged. The group rushed forward, coordinated in a struggle for survival. With a decisive thrust, the boar fell, its fight finally subdued. Silence settled over the forest, a calm that seemed to recognize their victory.

Jake stood there, chest heaving, yet something within him had changed—confidence growing. He was no longer just an observer lost in this landscape; he had acted decisively and made a difference.

He looked around at the tribe—their eyes reflecting not just respect but acceptance. In their gaze, he found validation and belonging that had eluded him until now. His mind buzzed: relief at succeeding where he had feared failure; pride in proving himself capable beyond coding and logic; gratitude for Amna's guidance and Tharik's trust.

In that moment beneath the canopy of leaves, Jake understood this was more than surviving another day—it was stepping into a role far greater than anything he had imagined back home.

The forest exhaled as the tribe gathered around the boar. Its massive form lay still, blood seeping into the earth, the clearing transformed in muted silence. The air shifted, carrying the scent of victory and the heaviness of life and death. The warriors lowered their spears, and the birds' cries slowly returned. The soft rustling of leaves seemed like the forest itself coming back to life.

Jake breathed deeply, chest still heaving with the remnants of adrenaline. He could feel the burn in his legs, the tremors in his arms. Around him, the tribe moved with purposeful calm, transitioning from chaos to ritual. There was no rush. This was the way of things. Survival, done with reverence.

Elder Kori moved with a grace that surprised those who knew her age, her presence demanding respect as both Elder and Shaman. She preserved their traditions and served as the spiritual leader with the wisdom of generations. As she knelt by the fallen boar, her hand rested gently on its side. She spoke in the ancient language—a prayer or invocation—her voice carrying the weight of history. The hunters lowered their heads. Jake followed their lead, unsure of the words but sensing the importance. This wasn't just about the kill; it was part of the cycle Elder Kori protected with her knowledge and guidance.

The tribe's ritual wasn't just about death—it was about respect. About balance.

Jake swallowed, eyes lowering, and felt the enormity of what he'd just been a part of. This tribe didn't see the world as something to conquer, but to coexist with.

When Elder Kori rose, her gaze found Jake's. No caution now. No wariness. Only something far deeper: recognition.

"You chose the path. You completed the rites. You did not run from the beast," she said, words soft but firm, carrying a weight Jake hadn't expected.

She didn't say more. But she didn't need to.

Amna appeared at his side, steady presence grounding him. She didn't speak either, but her silence spoke volumes—waiting for him to process, waiting for him to understand the trials had changed something in him. He realized, with a sudden shock, that they had.

Jake opened his mouth to say something—anything—but the words didn't come. Pride? Relief? No. Something he'd never fully allowed himself to feel before: belonging.

The firelight glimmered in the distance, casting long shadows. The tribe began to prepare the boar for transport, each movement precise, each gesture deliberate. Jake could feel something bigger than himself pulling him along.

Amna noticed his hesitation. Her lips quirked slightly, just a hint of a smile.

"The boar's spirit will speak of you," she said softly, watching as the others began to work.

Jake's mind whirred. Spirits had always felt foreign to him, like something out of a story. But the quiet conviction in her voice made him pause.

"Do spirits... usually talk about strangers?" he asked, quieter than he intended.

Amna pivoted to meet his eyes directly, expression piercing. When she spoke, the impact was more profound than he'd anticipated. In that instant, he realized how much more of their language he had absorbed since the trials—perhaps their true purpose all along.

"You were not a stranger."

The weight of those words landed heavily in his chest. Not a compliment. A declaration.

"You listened," she continued. "You learned. You moved as one of us. Even when afraid."

Jake lowered his eyes—not from shame, but from the weight of what she'd given him. Belonging.

The procession back to the village was slow, almost meditative. The hunters carried the boar's weight between them easily. Jake offered to help; his muscles protested, but he didn't hesitate. Tharik nodded at him, approval flickering in his sharp eyes. Together, they lifted the boar, the strain in Jake's shoulders a real, tangible connection to this world. Heavy. But worth it.

As they walked, the forest no longer felt like an enemy. It was a language he was learning—one word at a time, one trial at a time.

Amna glanced over, not critical, but thoughtful. Not to judge—only to understand. Jake caught something in her gaze—a flicker of interest, a curiosity that felt almost like an invitation.

"That thing you did," she said suddenly. "With the stones."

Jake looked up, surprised.

"You mean solving them?" he asked, half-smiling.

She nodded, unreadable. "You saw meaning in the shapes. As if they spoke to you."

Jake smiled, feeling lighter. "They kind of did," he admitted. "Patterns. Logic. That's how my mind works."

Amna's brow furrowed, intrigued. "Your world... it runs on this logic?"

Jake hesitated. "Sometimes. But sometimes it doesn't. Sometimes it runs on chaos, like anything else."

They fell into step beside each other, the silence stretching between them not awkward, but thoughtful—natural.

Amna looked at him again. "You still look," she said, "as if you're waiting for something."

Jake glanced at her, puzzled. "Like what?"

"Like the trial is not over," she said, quieter now.

He didn't answer. Because a part of him agreed. There was still something out there. Still something waiting—something that hadn't shown itself yet. The trial... it was just the beginning. The threshold, not the end.

The village fires glowed ahead, casting flickering shadows into the growing dusk. The murmurs rose, faces turning toward him as he approached. But this time it was different. No one looked away. No one doubted. No one questioned.

As Jake and Amna walked through the village, she pointed out individuals, sharing their names and roles. "That's Larek," she said, nodding toward a man weaving a basket so tight the reeds squeaked under his fingers. "He's our master craftsman."

As they passed an elderly woman with kind eyes crushing herbs with a smooth river stone, releasing a sharp green scent into the air, Amna added, "Elder Muna—our healer and wise guide."

A child waved at them enthusiastically before scampering off, and Elder Muna tapped a fingertip of ash to the child's forehead like a blessing before shooing them back to play. Approaching the woman adorned in beads who had once regarded Jake with stern stoicism, Amna explained, "This is Nalia." Nalia lifted a small rattle of bone and shell, testing its clack against the firelight as if listening for the right sound, then lowered it again without looking away.

"She oversees the rituals and ensures harmony among us." As they continued walking, Amna shared her own role as a mediator between tradition and change, helping Jake understand what he could expect from each villager.

Jake let it in. Not pride. But acceptance.

Amna leaned in closer, voice low, almost conspiratorial. "Tomorrow, there will be questions. Challenges. Perhaps more trials."

"Of course there will," Jake replied, voice steady, feeling the weight of what was to come.

"But tonight," she added, a faint smile tugging at the corner of her lips, "you are one of us."

Jake met her gaze, mind racing with possibilities—with thoughts of home and Emma, of what was next. He smiled back, genuine and unguarded.

"Then tonight," he said, "I'll stop waiting."

And for the first time since stepping through the portal, Jake didn't feel like a visitor. He didn't feel like an outsider. He felt like he belonged. And in that moment, the future—whatever it held—seemed wide open.

They sat on a fallen log beneath the dusk-lit canopy, the fire between them casting gold across Amna's face. Her eyes, sharp and thoughtful, flicked between the flame and Jake's fumbling attempts to copy her words.

"Sho'tari," she said again, slower this time. She touched her mouth, then her chest.

Jake mirrored her. "Sho'tari," he repeated. "Speak. Me."

She nodded once—not praise, not condescension. Just affirmation.

Jake smiled a little, then traced a line in the dirt. He drew a square, then a circle beside it. "In my world," he said slowly, "we use these to talk. Not mouths—machines."

Amna tilted her head. She tapped the circle. "Sun?"

He laughed softly. "Close. In code—zero."

"Zee-roh," she echoed, uncertain.

They sat in silence a moment, the crackle of fire filling the gaps where words failed. Jake glanced up, catching her watching him—not with suspicion, but curiosity.

"You... not afraid of me?" he asked, gesturing to himself.

Amna paused. "Not fear. Caution," she said. "You fall from storm. Speak strange. Carry mind in box." She nodded at The Bridge.

Jake nodded, embarrassed and amused. "Yeah. Box mind."

She studied him a beat longer. "But you... listen. Try. That means more than box."

The statement landed with weight. Jake looked at the fire, heart warming in a way the flames couldn't explain. "You're the first person who's said that."

"Then your people are poor with eyes," Amna replied softly.

He looked up. A faint smile ghosted her lips—small, but real.

Jake didn't speak after that. He just sat with her, firelight moving between logic and instinct, box and heart—two voices slowly learning how to share the same song.

Chapter 5:
Whispers of War

A few days later, dawn rose in thin, uncertain strands like a cautious promise, barely pushing past the edge of the clearing. Beyond it, the forest devoured the light in layers of shadow, as if nature itself were withholding the day. The village lay nestled in a protected basin, surrounded by dense woods that cut the horizon. Low huts, made from mud bricks and thatched with straw, clustered together, chimneys puffing faint wisps of smoke into the cool morning air. The village was simple but functional, a reflection of the rhythm and purpose of its people. Its perimeter was marked by a rough wooden stockade, reinforced with sharpened stakes, and guarded by crude stone towers built into the trees—enough to ward off larger threats, like wild animals and raiding parties from rival tribes.

But this—this was different.

Tharik crouched low on the muddy trail at the edge of the village, his eyes narrowed at the imprint on the ground. A footprint. Fresh. The surrounding area was quiet, but something about the silence felt too still, too deliberate. His fingers traced the shape of the print in the earth—a boot, smaller than a warrior's but still intentional, a sign of someone who knew the land. The edges were clean, not washed away by rain or disturbed by wind. And there—a thin, gridded tread—perfect little squares inside squares—like a mark made by a tool, not an uncovered foot. Someone had been here recently.

Tharik didn't move immediately. His mind ticked through possibilities. He had been patrolling this perimeter for days now, keeping an eye out for the strange occurrences that had been happening. The village's usual tranquility had been shattered by unspoken tension. The elders had spoken of dangers lurking beyond the trees—and now, with these tracks, it seemed that danger had arrived.

The weight of responsibility had been heavier since Jake's trials—Jake, the outsider who had passed the tests but remained a mystery.

Since the trials—since the boar hunt—there had been a shift. Some had begun to trust Jake, though the elders still watched carefully. His presence was still a point of contention. Some whispered doubts about the technology he carried, about the knowledge he claimed to have from another time.

Jake had been living in a modest hut near the outskirts of the village, given a place of honor despite his outsider status—safe, but separate. It was an unspoken acknowledgment of what he was: proven, but not quite one of them.

As Tharik observed the footprints, urgency pressed against him.

He signaled the other hunters silently, a sharp gesture that made the men spring into motion. Without a word, they scattered, moving through the forest with fluid control. The mist was thick, the air damp and cool as they pushed deeper into the woods. The sky above was gray, and the trees were hushed, holding secrets of their own.

Tharik moved with them, eyes scanning the ground for more prints, more signs of intrusion. Then—movement up ahead. A glimpse. A quick slip between trees. The markings were unmistakable: the twisted symbols of Malik's tribe.

Tharik's heart tightened. Malik's scouts. Here. Now.

The chase intensified.

Tharik signaled again. The hunters responded without hesitation, bodies cutting through the brush like spears. Their breath puffed white in the morning chill. They were closing in.

Tharik glimpsed the scout once more—a flicker of Malik's markings slipping behind a tree. The scout moved with purpose, weaving in and out of the trunks, but it was too late. The hunters were on him now.

He took a leap toward the ridge—a desperate move.

Tharik halted, eyes narrowing. The ridge was jagged, steep, and led into an area they didn't patrol often. A boundary they didn't know well. The scout's leap took him beyond their reach, deeper into unfamiliar terrain.

Tharik knew they couldn't follow. The fog was thick, the landscape treacherous. He shouted, sharp and commanding, cutting through the trees—a warning and a call. The village had to be told before this became something worse.

The sound ripped through the morning, a harsh cry that rolled like thunder across the waking woods. The hunters pivoted at once, tracking back toward the village. Tharik didn't need to look at them to know they understood. They were bound to protect their home.

As they returned, the village came into view. The perimeter defenses were still intact, but the air itself felt thick. The hunters broke through the tree line into the clearing, scattering villagers and drawing surprised eyes. Tharik was already barking orders, voice slicing through confusion.

"Malik's scouts!"

The name crashed into the camp like a thrown spear. Fear turned to motion. Weapons were seized. The village snapped awake.

From chaos, order rose. Tharik moved through the swirl like a fixed point, directing with gestures that cut through the noise.

This was the storm's edge—and Tharik was the first to feel it.

By mid-morning, the sun had risen high enough to light the village with a soft, golden glow. The sky was clear, but the air still held the crisp chill of the night.

Across the clearing, villagers worked in a flurry—reinforcing tents, sharpening weapons, gathering children near their mothers in the center of the village. Those who were not hunters moved quickly to patch gaps in the stockade, tying branches into weak seams and bracing the boundary with whatever they had.

Elder Kori moved among them, offering quiet prayers; her voice a whisper of calm amid the preparations. As the village's shaman, she was keeper of the tribe's spiritual health, but the elders were more than that—repository, memory, law.

Jake stood on the edge of the gathering, posture tense. His place had been earned through the trials, but his methods still raised suspicion. Respect for his bravery. Wariness for what he carried.

Amna stood beside him. She didn't speak much now. The tension was palpable. The tribe was gearing up for something they hadn't faced in a long time: Malik's scouts.

Jake had studied the village's defenses for days. He'd noticed gaps in the perimeter—places the stockade could be breached, where sight-lines died too quickly. The tribe's strategies were strong, but predictable. They needed time. Warning. A breath before impact.

"We need to reinforce the perimeter," Jake declared, his voice slicing through the gathering like a blade. They stood huddled in the meeting hall, surrounded by flickering torchlight that cast long shadows across the ancient stone walls. Faces watched him—skepticism threaded with curiosity.

Some younger warriors glanced his way, curious but cautious. Amna gave him a silent nod. Others held back.

Jake stepped closer to the stockade to make his point. "We can't rely on these barriers alone," he said, gesturing at the rough fence, gaps wide enough to slip a hand through. "We need an early warning system—something that alerts us before the attack starts."

His mind ran through simple, effective methods—things he could build here, with what they had.

"Alarms," Jake continued. "Shells. String. Bones. Basic, but it'll work."

He crouched by the stockade and laid it out. "We tie shells or stones to string and set them around the perimeter. The slightest movement—like a footfall—will send them rattling. You can't see them in the dark, but you can hear them."

Warriors exchanged looks. The idea was simple enough to be unsettling—too easy, too foreign.

"And a whistle system," Jake added. "Different tones for different threats. Fast. Quiet. No panic."

Amna stepped forward then, voice firm. "If we wait, we will fall. We act now."

A murmur rippled through the younger warriors—still unsure, but listening.

Varun stepped into the circle just as Jake finished, his expression a carefully controlled mask of calm. At twenty, he was an ambitious disciple of Elder Kori, steeped in the shamanic traditions of the village—herbs, ritual, the old words. He was training to become the next shaman, and that training came with a hunger he didn't always hide. Jake's arrival had shifted attention in the village. Varun felt it. And envy had a way of turning into resentment.

The hours following the gathering were filled with rapid preparation. By the time dusk settled over the village, the air felt heavy with anticipation. Every villager had a role—every hand working toward a common purpose. Jake could feel the weight of the moment pressing against him, his mind constantly calculating, considering, planning. The village's defenses were rudimentary at best. The stockade, though sturdy, had its weak points—gaps between the branches and unguarded sections of the perimeter. But Jake had a few ideas to enhance what they had.

As night fell, the warriors, led by Tharik and Amna, worked with Jake to implement his plan. They set up basic alarm systems: strings of animal bones, shells, and stones tied to thin ropes were hidden along the perimeter. Each time someone stepped on them, they would rattle, sending an early warning to the hunters without them needing to see the intruder. Jake, unfamiliar with their old ways but eager to contribute, had also introduced a simple hand-signal communication system based on his own experiences with code and signaling techniques. The idea was simple: each gesture meant specific directions, numbers, or actions. It was something he had learned quickly in his own world.

It wasn't perfect, but the warriors were quick to adapt, understanding the usefulness of a system that didn't require shouting or verbal cues. The trick was making it as intuitive as possible, and they had a few hours to practice. At first, it was awkward—Jake gesturing, the warriors trying to mimic his signs. But by the time the perimeter was fully fortified, and the last traps were set, they had enough of a grasp on the system to respond to basic signals.

Jake's steadfast companion, The Bridge, rested warm against his ribs beneath his shirt—compact, rugged, no larger than a thick paperback. To the villagers it was sorcery: a sealed mind, a forbidden thing. To Jake it was a tether, a quiet line back to logic. Its charge had held steady for weeks, thanks to a thin solar panel integrated into its casing that drank sunlight whenever he stepped outside. Tonight, it did more than hum. It tracked trap placements, marked weak seams in the stockade, and mapped the warriors' positions in blunt, shifting symbols Jake could read at a glance. When the world narrowed to fog and footsteps, The Bridge kept his thinking sharp.

As the sun finally dipped below the horizon, a heavy fog rolled over the village—a natural cover that would have masked any incoming attack. The village itself was divided into clusters of huts and tents. The warriors were positioned on the outer perimeter, watching for any signs of movement. The non-combatants—women, children, and the elderly—were gathered inside the central village hall—a large, circular structure made of stone and mud. It was the most fortified structure in the village, with thick walls and a sturdy roof. Inside, Elder Kori kept vigil, offering spiritual guidance and preparing for the worst. The rest of the villagers had been given orders to stay close, to shelter in the hall or inside their homes if they could.

Jake, Amna, and Tharik had worked quickly to set an ambush, positioning warriors in the underbrush around the village, setting up traps near the less guarded points of the stockade, and leaving a few decoys to lure Malik's raiders in.

Jake wasn't a warrior, but he had learned enough about positioning, traps, and strategy to assist. His stone-tipped spear, a gift from one of the hunters, hung at his side, though he was determined not to fight unless absolutely necessary. He had learned to throw it with some skill, but the warriors had made it clear—his strength was in his mind, not in combat.

It was almost an hour before the attack came. The first sign of movement came from the outer perimeter—one of the alarms went off with a sharp rattle. Then another. Tharik, stationed at the northeast corner of the village, signaled to Jake with a series of quick, precise hand gestures. Jake's heart quickened, but he didn't hesitate. His eyes scanned the perimeter from where he stood near the village hall, watching for signs of Malik's scouts.

Then the real sound came—far off at first, like distant thunder rolling over the hills. The raiders had breached the stockade at the southeast corner. It wasn't loud, no great crash or breach, but the soft, steady movement of bodies slipping through the gaps. The warriors had missed the signs.

Tharik's voice rang out, sharp and commanding, breaking the silence. "They're inside!"

Panic could have easily swept over the village, but Jake's quick thinking and the warriors' prior training steadied the group. They moved into action, their movements synchronized despite the chaos. The villagers were not fighters, but the warriors had drilled them in what to do in case of an attack. They scrambled to the village hall, gathering what weapons they could, prepared to defend their home.

Jake's heart pounded, his mind racing. He raised his hand and signaled to the warriors in the field with a set of sharp gestures. The response was swift—warriors crouched low, moving through the brush, flanking the raiders from multiple sides. Jake's coding rig helped him track the movement of the warriors, allowing him to adjust the plan on the fly. He could see where they were falling into position, where the gaps were in the defenses, and what needed to be adjusted in real time. It wasn't a perfect system, but it was enough to give them an edge.

Malik's warriors began to surge into the village, unaware of the traps that had been laid for them. The warriors hidden in the forest leaped into action, springing the traps as they were triggered. Shells rattled loudly, signaling their positions, and the warriors fired arrows from the trees. A handful of Malik's scouts were caught off guard, their confidence faltering. They tried to regroup, but the confusion worked against them. They weren't expecting such a well-organized defense.

In the chaos, Amna took her place, charging headlong into the fray, her stone blade flashing in the moonlight. Her presence was a rallying cry for the warriors, her leadership a steadying force in the storm of confusion. Jake watched her with admiration, but he knew his place wasn't on the front lines. He wasn't a fighter.

He moved through the confusion, issuing hand signals to the warriors stationed in the village and outside, guiding them toward the raiders' positions. The traps he had set worked exactly as planned. A few more of Malik's men were caught in snares, their weapons dropped as they struggled. As the attackers began to retreat, the warriors tightened their grip, pushing them back toward the stockade of fallen trees and rocks mixed in with mud.

Jake's thoughts were a blur, his body tense as he directed the battle. His mind, always used to calculating systems, found clarity in the chaos. This was his domain. The simulations he'd once run in his own world had prepared him for moments like this. Except this wasn't a game. This was real, and it was working.

When the first wave of Malik's warriors retreated, Tharik nodded at Jake across the battlefield, his expression hard but approving. The village was holding. The traps had worked. The warriors had fought with skill and determination, and the tribe's unity had turned the tide.

Malik's men began to scatter, retreating into the forest; their plans disrupted. They hadn't expected the village to fight back like this, and now they were on the defensive. The remaining villagers began to chant in victory, their fear dissipating into the air.

As the last of the raiders disappeared into the woods, Jake stood there, heart still racing, body tight with leftover adrenaline. Amna approached, her face alive with fierce pride.

"They thought us weak," she said.

Jake could only nod. He wasn't a warrior—but today he had been something else. A strategist. A pivot point.

Across the camp, a villager stared at him like he'd done magic. "You knew," they said.

Jake shook his head. "I knew they'd try."

Tharik appeared at his shoulder, expression unchanged—eyes sharp with approval. "Well done, Jake," he said simply.

Even Varun held his tongue. He had seen the plan work.

Amna moved closer, and when she spoke again, it wasn't a hopeful wish. It was a certainty.

"They'll see."

Jake stood quietly by the fire, The Bridge still warm against his side. Relief spread through the village in uneven waves—laughter, chants, the release of fear.

Then The Bridge beeped.

A warning flashed.

Jake's stomach dropped. He didn't read it as code. He read it as omen.

"Amna," he whispered. "Something's coming."

Without waiting for a response, he ran.

Chapter 6: The Storm Breaks

The sky above the village of sun-baked clay homes churned like a restless sea, dark and low, as if the heavens were folding inward. Jake stood in the open square, surrounded by people whose ancestors had walked this land for generations. He had moved through the village for days now, but he'd never felt so alien.

Elder Kori stood calmly at the center, her long silver hair braided with feathers and clay beads. Her presence was timeless, solid as stone. She lifted her hand and spoke—not loudly, but clearly enough to slice through the rising wind.

"When the heavens roar, hearts must decide."

The villagers reacted at once. Some fell to their knees, palms pressed to cracked earth, whispering to the ancestors. Others turned away, muttering that storms were common this season, that the gods had spoken before and would speak again. Jake's hand tightened around The Bridge, the compact device humming faintly with heat. Its display glowed dimly, symbols shifting like anxious fireflies.

He read the data again. Barometric pressure was crashing. Temperature spiked. Wind vectors fractured into impossible loops. Jake knew storms—he'd coded models for them—but this? The numbers were breaking. Repeating. As if something beneath the sky itself had slipped.

A group of villagers pushed past him, casting wary glances at the device. An older woman whispered a warding chant, fingers twitching in a gesture against evil. Voices rose. The sacred square pressed tighter.

Across the gathering, Amna met his eyes. Uncertainty flickered there—doubt, fear—but also the beginning of belief. She stepped forward.

"Amna!" Jake called, his voice snagging on the wind.

A gust tore dirt into the air. Branches bent and creaked. An elder raised a staff. "The spirits test our patience! Hold to the old ways!"

A younger man sneered near the grain store. "Let the gods speak through reason, not wind!"

The storm was no longer just above them. It had entered the people.

Jake glanced at The Bridge again. Static bled into the glyphs. This wasn't weather. Something was distorting the air itself.

"A storm is coming!" Jake shouted, climbing onto a low platform near the grain bins. "Not like the others. This one isn't natural!"

Young faces turned. Curious ones. Those who remembered the trials. Who had seen what he could fix.

The ground rippled beneath them—a faint quake, just enough to steal breath.

Then the animals fled. Goats tore loose from their ties. Birds exploded skyward in a frantic spiral.

"They'll pass us by!" someone shouted.

Jake knew they wouldn't.

Amna hesitated only a heartbeat before turning to the elders. "Sound the drums."

The alert rhythm boomed across the rooftops—warning and unity braided into one. From the lodge near the river bend, a boy struck the hollowed log. The sound carried. Doubt paused.

Then Varun stepped forward.

Clad in ocher and green, the shaman's disciple smiled thinly. "The outsider's magic hums and sputters," he said smoothly. "But does it know the spirits of this land? Or has it angered them?"

Jake didn't answer. He couldn't.

The sky lowered. The wind shifted.

And deep within The Bridge, a new signal emerged.

A pulse.

A pattern.

A warning.

It was nightfall, a day after Malik's raid when the storm hit.

The storm came with a scream.

Wind ripped through the square, hurling debris into the trees. Rain drove sideways—sharp and needling. Thunder split the sacred stone tree clean down the middle.

Jake shouted orders from the half-rebuilt lookout frame. Villagers ran. Hands bled. Some froze.

Amna cut through the chaos. "Do what he says! Now!"

Lightning struck close enough to explode soil into the air.

Jake dragged The Bridge free. Its glyphs spiraled, corrupted. The glow deepened—blue-violet, wrong.

"It's feedback," he muttered. "Full-spectrum—"

Another strike threw them flat.

They barely reached the great hall before the doors slammed shut.

And still, from his satchel, The Bridge hummed.

Morning came too slowly.

The storm had passed, but its ghost clung to everything. The silence afterward felt wrong—like breath held too long.

Jake stepped into the pale light beside Amna. The air reeked of smoke, wet ash, and earth.

The village was a ruin.

If Malik's raid had broken the surface, the storm had buried it.

The square had turned into a swamp of churned mud and broken bone. The huts—already scorched and weakened—now lay flattened or waterlogged. The longhouse roof had collapsed under a felled limb. Half the weapons were lost to the mire.

The sacred tree had split in half—its roots exposed like veins. Offerings floated beside it, half-burnt feathers and woven charms drifting in puddles.

Jake moved among the wreckage in silence.

Some villagers emerged. Some wept openly. Others looked to the sky, then to him.

Not with gratitude.

With fear.

Then Varun spoke. "This is your doing."

Amna stepped in. Others followed—quiet voices, living proof.

Elder Kori ended it with a raised hand. "Fear is the fire that eats from within."

The crowd did not split.

They cracked—and began to heal.

That night, Jake dreamed of storm-lit portals spiraling across the sky.

And a voice—older, rougher—whispered:

"This world remembers. You're not the first."

He woke cold and certain.

They feared him more than the storm.

He stared at the shattered square.

The night was still. Broken. Empty.

He dressed. Slipped outside. The village slept, but the destruction remained.

They feared him more than the storm.

He remembered his father's hands—steady, calm, building a tree house in a summer storm.

"Always a way," his father used to say.

He stared at the shattered square.

He would rebuild.

Wood. Wire.

Word by word.

Chapter 7: Seeds of Change

At the edge of the village, where worn paths surrendered to untamed wilderness, Jake crouched low, fingers tracing rough timber and jagged stone. It had been about a week since that unnatural storm followed Malik's brutal raid. The storm hadn't been just weather; it had felt alive—almost sentient, as if responding to something unseen. As dawn's first light slipped over the tree line, casting elongated shadows across the clearing, Jake replayed the moment it surged—right when his portable coding rig hummed to life. A coincidence he couldn't ignore.

Could his device—its quantum-based interface—have tapped something ancient? The charred remnants of shelters stood like silent witnesses around him. Smoke-scorched earth whispered tales not yet forgotten. Alone, Jake mulled theories: maybe his technology bridged realms beyond time and space, interacting with forces as old as the land itself. Or maybe it had been a warning from spirits entwined with nature—a call for balance disrupted by modern intrusions.

But this—this he could work with.

He spread tools across the soil—shaped wood, rope from tree bark, hand-carved stone tools—then dragged a line through the dirt with a pointed stick. Symbols. Shapes. Circuitry simplified to survive. Around him, a cluster of younger villagers stood silent, uncertain.

"It starts here," Jake said, sketching a loop. "Strong frame. Right tension. We don't force it—we fit it."

They didn't nod, but their silence leaned in.

He picked up knotted fiber and looped it through a support beam. "These materials—wood, stone, fiber—they're already smart. You just have to listen."

A boy shifted his weight. "This isn't how we build."

Jake kept weaving. "It's not how you used to build."

From the tree line, a shadow moved. Varun stepped into view, arms folded, eyes hard.

"Our way has lasted," he said. "Your tricks won't."

Jake didn't rise. He turned the loop again, precise. "Then we'll test them. If they fail, we'll know."

Varun said nothing. The younger ones didn't either.

"Can we keep both?" a girl asked. "His and ours?"

"Not a question of keeping," Jake replied. He drew an arch with anchor lines. "It's about growing."

Jake retrieved The Bridge from his pack, its surface dimly glowing with data—soil density, weight load, pressure tolerances. The device's energy was waning; the flicker was a warning. Without explaining, he adjusted the diagram on its screen. A curious boy crouched beside him, peering at the gadget. "What's that thing tell you?"

Jake handed him the stick. "That your land knows more than I do. Go on. Copy that curve."

They traced together. One by one, others joined. The sun climbed. By mid-morning, the clearing buzzed with low talk and the creak of bending wood.

When another boy fumbled the knot, Jake knelt beside him. "Pull there. Hold. See? The strength isn't in the rope—it's where you place the pressure."

The knot held. Whispers grew. Doubt thinned.

"This isn't ours yet," someone murmured.

"It's already yours," Jake said. "I'm just giving you new shapes to work with."

Varun's voice slashed through the air. "And when your shapes break?"

Jake met his stare. "Then we fix them. That's the part your way forgot—how to change."

Someone laughed. Uncertain, but real.

A girl pointed. "That one looks like our old traps. Just... wider."

"Exactly," Jake nodded. "Old bones. New skin."

Varun didn't answer. But he didn't leave either.

Jake wiped his hands, eyes sweeping the site—timber, a thin strand of copper thread scavenged from his pack, young minds catching fire.

"You want to know if it works?" Jake asked.

No reply.

"Then help me build it."

He held Varun's stare. No one walked away.

The village had started to shift. Not with blueprints, but with questions. With hands in the dirt.

The sun rose over the horizon, stretching its rays through the misty clearing. Light danced off dewdrops and glistened on sweating backs. The wooden frame was nearly complete, curved supports and tight joints settling into place.

Jake strained as he lifted the side of a heavy beam, muscles burning. Around him, villagers called out, their voices mixing with construction and the constant rustle of the forest. Sweat streaked down his back, soaking his tunic. Timber groaned. Rope tightened with the threat of snapping.

"Hold there!" Jake called, urgency underscoring his words. "Shift weight to the right—now! If it tilts, we lose everything."

Hands scrambled. The beam locked into place, and Jake felt the tension shift—effort turning into something solid. Cheers broke out across the clearing, sending energy through the team. For a moment, everyone let out a collective breath. Jake wiped his brow and grinned through the fatigue.

He moved from team to team, offering guidance. A girl lashed supports with finesse, fiber looping like she'd done it forever. A boy wedged braces beneath a slanted post, brow furrowed. Jake knelt beside him, calm authority growing in him.

"Lower," he advised, demonstrating with his hands. "Use the pressure, not balance."

The boy adjusted. The post straightened—solid and true—and his face broke into a smile. Jake watched designs spread over the earth like a second skin: curved supports, tension-tested joints, balance walking the line between instinct and numbers.

New didn't replace old. It strengthened it. That was the point.

This fusion reignited a familiar spark in Jake. It was the essence of innovation, the heart of every project he'd ever obsessed over. But here it meant more. It was connection.

He watched the young villagers, eyes bright with discovery. Their curiosity mirrored his—shared pursuit crossing any boundary of time.

His thoughts snapped back when he noticed Varun standing apart.

Varun circled the site, watching. Finally he said, loud enough to stop hands mid-motion, "This isn't building. It's guessing."

Jake looked up, unfazed. "It's engineering. Different word. Same result."

Varun stepped closer. "You make them forget what they carry. What they owe."

Jake shook his head. "I'm not asking them to forget. I'm trying to build something that won't collapse in the next storm."

"Our shelters lasted," Varun insisted. Then, sharper: "Yours haven't been tested."

Jake assessed the wall rising. "Then test them," he said.

The young builders pushed against the wall with their combined strength. It held. A cheer erupted, cracking the tension. Jake couldn't help but grin.

"Again," he called. "Bigger."

The air shifted. Determination caught fire.

A loud crack rang out. A beam snapped. The wall wobbled dangerously.

Jake reacted instantly. "Shift left! Take the pressure off!"

They moved as one. The frame stabilized. Relief washed over them.

"Mistakes aren't the end," Jake said. "It's how we adjust."

Varun pointed, trying to cut him down. "That's your way: fail, then explain."

"No," Jake replied. "Learn, then improve." He stepped into the center, voice steady. "Every mistake you ever learned from? Someone made it first."

A boy stepped forward, determination blazing. "Then let me make one."

Jake handed him a tool. The moment held—a weight of trust.

"Do it," Jake said.

The boy knelt. Others joined. Rhythm returned—stronger.

By afternoon, a new structure stood tall. Timber and fiber braided into a framework that didn't just hold weight—it held hope.

As dusk fell, the village glowed with firelight. Jake's mind buzzed. The work wasn't just physical. It tied them together.

The first stars appeared. Bonfires flickered and threw their light across the new builds. Laughter mingled with crackling wood. Jake stood amid it all—tired, satisfied, present in a way the digital world had never given him.

A young woman approached, face half-lit by fire. "I never thought we'd see this," she said, looking at the sturdy frames. "The tribe's never built like this."

Jake smiled, nodding. "We did it." And he meant it—collective, shared.

Varun lingered at the edge, tense and shadowed, still watching. But people clustered closer to Jake. Children ran in circles. Young workers clapped each other's backs, earlier doubts thinning into pride.

"Jake, look! We built this!"

Jake laughed, ruffling hair, taking their joy as proof they'd claimed it. Not just structures—possibility.

A small voice whispered, "Thank you."

Jake knelt to meet the boy's eyes. "We showed each other," he said.

At the edge of the clearing, Amna sat alone, shoulders hunched, staring past the firelight. In her lap lay her father's necklace, her fingers wrapped around it.

Jake hesitated. He hadn't seen her hold it since the raid. Her father had been one of the casualties, protecting the village when Malik struck. Firelight flickered over carved beads and feathered cord. Jake hadn't mentioned him. He'd respected her silence.

A memory flashed: Emma in the yard, drawing symbols in the dirt. *You always act like everything's code.*

Because it is.

But you never debug yourself.

Those words hit now, harder than any critique.

Behind him, Varun's voice broke the quiet. "The old ways won't be forgotten."

Jake didn't turn. His focus stayed on Amna. "They'll grow stronger," he said.

As night wore on, the village fell toward sleep. Fires burned low. Embers mirrored the stars.

Late into the night, the village was wrapped in gentle silence. Most had drifted off, emptied by work and celebration. Embers glowed feebly, throwing long shadows across the clearing. Only wind in the trees moved.

On the outskirts, Jake sat alone, thoughts circling. Beside him lay The Bridge, its lights dim, flickering like a weak heartbeat.

It had been a blur since the wall rose—and since Amna gave him the necklace. She'd handed it over quietly, serious, like it mattered beyond words. Jake had tucked it into hide and bark, feeling its presence like a question that wouldn't stop asking.

Curiosity won. He connected the sensor and pressed it carefully against the stone disc.

The necklace was smooth azure stone, coin-small, etched with intricate spirals. Under moonlight it shimmered, almost alive, as if the patterns shifted. The leather cord was worn but strong—survival disguised as fragility.

A faint hum rose from the disc. Not sound exactly—pressure. Like a frequency just under hearing.

Jake watched the scanner output.

SIGNATURE DETECTED.

TIMESTAMP ANOMALY... MULTIPLE ITERATIONS.

IDENTITY FRAGMENT: E.

The letter lodged in his mind like a splinter.

Emma.

The embers seemed to dim. The world narrowed.

Then—a fragmented voice, thin under static:

"Jake... if you're reading this, then you're already too close to the fracture. I tried to warn you. I—"

Static. Silence.

Jake tapped to replay. Nothing came back—only the oppressive quiet.

He barely noticed footsteps until they stopped beside him.

Amna stood there, watching with a mix of curiosity and concern.

Jake didn't look up. "Do you know her name?" he asked.

Amna paused, sorting memory and story. "She said one word," she said softly. "It sounded like yours."

Jake's grip tightened around the disc. The letter. The voice. The warning. The shape of it all.

"You buried it," Amna said, glancing at the necklace.

"To protect it," Jake replied, and realized he meant it.

Amna sat beside him, eyes catching the last firelight. "My father spoke of her arrival during the Long Night," she said, her tone shifting—legend carried like breath.

The Long Night: when darkness hung over the land and even the stars vanished. A visitor came. Then vanished. No one understood her meaning. But she left something behind.

"Is she the traveler?" Jake asked, the theory forming before he could stop it.

Amna nodded. "She said someone would return. Someone caught between the stars and time. They would need this."

The stone vibrated faintly in Jake's hand, answering him in a way that made his skin prickle.

"She said a name," Amna whispered. "It sounded like yours."

Jake had no words. Decades of story collapsed into a single point.

Emma had been here.

Not just a gift.

A warning. A guide.

And on the underside of the disc, the scanner caught a second trace—a clean, repeating tag pattern that looked wrong in this era. Not organic. Not spirit. A signature formatted like a manufacturer's stamp.

For a second, The Bridge tried to resolve it—then the display scrambled, as if something didn't want to be named.

Jake swallowed.

Something had touched this.

Something *made* contact.

The sky began to pale. The fire had turned to coals. Thin smoke rose from the central hearth as breakfast fires sparked. Roasted tubers and drying meat drifted on the breeze. Soon the village would gather. Elders worked efficiently, pressing grain into flatbread. Mothers banked coals into flame. Hunters stretched, checked spears, sharpened blades. Scouts slipped beyond the edge, eyes on ridgelines.

Jake settled onto a sun-warmed rock. Amna joined him, and the silence between them was thick with what they hadn't said.

After a while, Amna asked if the girl he'd mentioned was his sister.

He nodded slowly. "My sister. Thirteen. Curious. Too curious sometimes."

Amna ran her fingers over the necklace. "She left this for you," she said, holding the disc up to the light.

"Or for the version of me who never made it back," Jake replied, and heard the grief in his own voice.

"She came here on purpose?" Amna asked.

Jake hesitated. "No." Then, quieter: "Or... maybe she did. Maybe she knew something I didn't."

Amna watched him. "Why didn't she stay?"

Jake's voice wavered. "Because she's trying to stop something. And if she stayed... maybe she couldn't."

He looked down at the disc. "This isn't just jewelry. It's a message."

Amna drew her knees up, studying him. "Your situation is unusual."

Jake managed a faint smile. "So is yours. But we're both part of it now."

Amna turned, eyes bright with resolve. "Do we follow her trail?"

Jake looked east, where light touched the horizon. "No," he said. "We follow the fracture. She's already ahead. We have to catch up."

He secured the disc in his pocket, sealing the decision.

The Bridge gave a soft chime—too clean, too precise.

And for a beat, Jake could've sworn the chime carried a second tone beneath it—like an answering ping, distant, patient... listening.

Chapter 8: The Price of Knowledge

Three full moons had passed since the storm.

In the early morning, the village had risen from ruin like bone from mud—tentative, but solid. In the pale breath of dawn, mist tangled through the tall stone pines, and dew kissed the thatched roofs of mud-brick huts.

Jake rose before dawn, joining the hunters' patrol tasked with safeguarding the village. His route traced the outer ridge, a vigilant path that wound back through storage lanes where the bounty of their recent innovations lay in wait: woven nets cradling dried meat, lined clay barrels brimming with grain. Nearby, stone-tipped spears and axes glinted under early light—edges crafted from scavenged obsidian, bone, and sharpened iron scraps, balanced for use.

Each knot, post, and lash received his attention. Jake's mind scanned the perimeter the way his code once traced anomalies—input, process, output, iterate. Hidden behind the fire circle under a reed-covered lean-to, The Bridge rested silent. Its faint blue glow had flickered briefly the night the necklace reacted—but since then, nothing. No pulses. No signals.

But something still pressed against his thoughts—Emma's presence, coded in his neurons like a phantom subroutine waiting to run.

Not now. Not with what's coming.

A boy with long arms struggled to drag a wooden crate toward the tree line.

"Too far," Jake called, sharp. "Pull it in—east ridge, inside the traps."

The boy paused, glanced at the dense woods as if something might lurch out, then nodded and adjusted his course. Jake moved on.

Two teens fumbled with a spear bundle. The rope slipped.

"Tighter," Jake barked. "Split the load if you have to."

One narrowed his eyes with irritation. The other offered a weary nod, fingers roughened by endless toil. Jake pressed on. Seeking approval was no longer his goal; survival was. Three moons ago, he had been an outsider peering into a world of ancient customs and primal rhythms. Now, he moved through the village with belonging forged in necessity.

Makeshift shelters had become sturdier structures reinforced with woven branches and mud bricks, their shapes echoing the land. Fields surrounding the village teemed with vitality; crops sown in careful rows stretched toward the sun. Irrigation channels carved from earth and simple pulley systems for lifting water had turned barren patches into thriving gardens. Weapons lay ready for defense, their edges honed by hands that once knew only peace.

Emma's message lingered—time slipping away. He needed to stabilize the village, not just for their sake but to unravel the clues leading him home. Each day brought new challenges, a delicate balance keeping him tethered between worlds yet rooted in this one.

A young scout raced up, panting. "We're ready," he said. "Orders?"

"Link with the tree-line sentries. Look for soft spots. Move quickly."

The scout peeled off. Around Jake, the village shifted—warriors sparred near the center ring, elders passed like silent sentinels, bone necklaces clinking faintly, feathered hats turning with judgment.

Jake remembered Malik's last raid—the broken homes, the screams.

He crossed to the weapons area where artisans tested stone axes, balancing them with wrapped plant-fiber grips. Jake crouched, adjusted a weight ratio, and nodded. Elder Muna watched from behind a sharpened tusk. Her eyes narrowed.

"Will your tricks make them forget how to fight?" she asked, voice like dry bark.

Jake met her gaze. "No. They'll make sure they live long enough to remember how."

Muna grunted but didn't object.

A shadow fell. Tharik stepped forward.

"Do you question him?" he asked, arms crossed over his fur-wrapped chest. "His traps fed us through the rains. His rig saved two scouts last moon."

The elders said nothing. But their silence wasn't rejection.

Jake turned to Tharik. "We need overlapping patrols—double eyes along the south ridge."

"Scouts aren't hawks," Tharik muttered.

"Then they'll move like foxes. I'll test two squads. We'll see who adapts."

Tharik grunted approval—a low sound like stone grinding. Respect, not agreement. Yet.

Jake sliced a signal in the air. Scouts split off, fast and focused. The village, once hesitant, now moved like a network—tasks divided, motion synchronized.

Then—crunch. Fast footsteps behind.

A scout burst into view. "They're coming. From the cliffs. Fast."

Jake didn't pause.

Tharik fell in beside him. "Distance?"

"Less than the way to the herd on the horizon."

Jake snapped, "West line. Go!"

The village became fluid motion—elders shouting, children whisked into inner huts, weapons lifted. Drums pounded a hard rhythm.

Jake and Tharik sprinted through the trees. At the forest's edge, Jake adjusted a spike trigger and set a snare.

He turned to Tharik. "Time's short."

"We finish this."

The trees breathed, bristling. Distant drums. Then—figures in the mist.

Jake gripped his spear. "Let's see what they've got."

Tharik cracked a grin. "Let's see what you've got."

And the enemy arrived.

Smoke hung thick among the branches. From the cliffs and ridge, Malik's warriors emerged—bodies coated in ash and ochre, eyes glinting like dark stones. They approached quiet at first, then louder as dawn broke.

Jake was alert before he could even see them. Twigs snapped. Low growls carried. Birds burst upward in frantic spirals.

Then came the charge—clubs, flint-tipped spears, sharpened bone. They surged forward with primal force.

"Hold the line!" Jake shouted.

This time, the villagers listened.

They held, backs to the village, shields raised—thick bark and hide. In front of them lay Jake's traps, hidden beneath greenery. As Malik's warriors charged, vine snares snapped up, sending attackers tumbling. Pitfalls opened beneath feet. Bone-carved spikes kicked upward—deadly, precise, triggered by concealed mechanisms. Nets dropped from branches. Pressure branches buried in leaves caught legs and throats.

The villagers had never been this prepared.

Before Jake, they reacted to attacks chaotically—fleeing, screaming, flames. Now they had defenses, coordinated patrols, and signals using smoke and drumbeats. Basic, but organized. Logical.

Malik noticed.

He stood on the rise beyond the trees, calm amid chaos. Wind tugged his fur wrap. A bone mask shaped like a menacing cat covered half his face. His visible eye gleamed with hunger and calculation.

He had lived high in the mountains once—thin air, cold stone, wild beasts. His people hunted and herded. Then the ice receded. The herds vanished. Famine drove them down into the lowlands, and Malik survived by conquering unprotected settlements.

Jake's village hadn't crumbled. It fortified. It fought back.

Malik blamed the outsider for their resilience.

This boy was a threat. The boy with the glowing fire.

Malik couldn't comprehend it. It flashed in the dark and sang its high-pitched call softly in the stillness. When it blazed, everything shifted—warriors moved sharper, traps bit harder, time felt... wrong.

I will have it, or it will burn.

Jake moved along the defenders, searching for weakness.

"Fall back two steps! Brace the middle!"

They adjusted seamlessly. They did not falter.

Tharik appeared relentless, streaked with dirt and blood, stone axe swinging. "We can drive them back! Push!"

Encouraged, the villagers advanced—spears thrusting, clubs swinging, resistance rising into a brutal cadence.

Jake spotted a young girl drop her staff. She snatched a fallen spear and drove it forward. Fear widened her eyes, but her grip stayed steady.

More traps fired. More cries. Surprise rippled through Malik's line.

Yet some warriors slipped through, dodging snares that should've caught them.

How?

Jake snapped to the rear. "East side—reinforce the snare line! Protect the opening by the old boar path!"

Tharik roared back.

Then Jake saw Malik—still watching, not moving, not afraid.

Jake's hand went to his satchel. The Bridge lay hidden, faintly warm, almost sensing Malik's gaze.

"Tharik!" Jake shouted. "Over there! It's him!"

Tharik didn't look. "Don't break ranks. That's what he wants."

Jake's pulse climbed as Malik lifted a heavy staff, blackened and tipped with mammoth horn.

"Fall back!" Malik shouted.

His warriors withdrew in near perfect unison—not fear, strategy.

Tharik's face twisted. "We chase them!"

Jake's instincts screamed against it, but Tharik surged forward. Others followed, crashing through branches, bypassing traps, expecting the next wave.

There was nothing.

Only silence, acrid smoke, fading footprints.

Jake stood in the clearing, hands shaking, blood and ash on his skin. Around him, villagers turned toward him—gratitude, awe, something like relief.

You kept us alive.

Jake spoke low and rough. "This was only the start."

Tharik returned from the tree line, sweat and blood marking his face. "And we're still here."

Smoke still curled through broken branches. Midday sun pressed high. The heat wasn't the problem—sweat evaporated before it reached Jake's jaw, leaving salt and grit. They had survived, but the cost sat heavy.

The outer perimeter was in disarray. Traps were triggered. Bark shields cracked. Hide tents slashed. Warriors limped by. Children cried, small voices cutting the air. Healers moved fast, but boiled moss paste and bark poultices ran low. Jake moved slowly, not from pain, but from the weight of what came next.

They'd fought better than ever. Still, he couldn't shake how close it had been.

He passed the well. A boy barely six clutched a bandaged wrist. No tears—just a heavy silence.

Near the southern line, Tharik spoke with the elders. Their posture had shifted. They had once turned their backs on Jake's ideas. Now they leaned in. Listening.

Jake didn't join them. Instead, he went to the central hut that had become his by default. Inside, The Bridge rested on folded hides. Beside it hung the stone-disc necklace, catching light just right. Spiral markings glowed faintly blue.

Jake crouched, retrieved the necklace, and plugged the hide-wrapped copper tendril into The Bridge.

The screen shimmered—weak but steady. He brought the disc near the inlet port and keyed a diagnostic pattern.

SIGNAL DETECTED. PARTIAL MATCH. TEMPORAL DISPLACEMENT: 68%.

Jake's heart kicked. The signal wasn't close or recent, but it was there.

He closed his eyes and heard Emma, soft and maddeningly clear: *Maybe it's not a system. Maybe it's a story.*

He pocketed the necklace and stepped outside. The heaviness in his chest wasn't only battle fatigue; it was uncertainty.

At the forest's edge, he found a snare he'd designed. Disabled—not tripped. Disarmed.

A chill crawled his spine.

Jake scanned faces, searching. Varun hadn't been near the fight, the wounded, or the elders. And some of Malik's warriors had slipped traps too cleanly. The snares meant to hold them had been left untied.

This wasn't chance.

He found Tharik crouched by a net-snare. "You disappeared," Tharik said, still working.

"Had to check on something," Jake replied, urgency slipping through.

"Important?" Tharik asked.

Jake looked toward the trees. "Maybe too important."

They worked in silence. Tharik's hands tied knots with practiced ease. Then he asked, quieter, "Is that necklace... Emma's?"

"Yeah," Jake said, and something like pride rose despite everything. "She always finds a way to leave her mark."

Tharik nodded. "Most just vanish without a trace. But she left you something to hold on to—a path."

Jake stared into the gathering shadow of the forest, thinking of failed traps and the possibility of sabotage.

Varun's absence loomed. Malik had been too informed.

By nightfall, celebration had bled out into a heavy hush. Fires were snuffed in haste. Huts repaired with damp hides. Children whispered instead of laughed. Warriors stared at their hands too long after sharpening spears.

They'd survived Malik's latest raid, but three had fallen that morning: two hunters and a young girl, Alira, struck down while carrying water. Her mother hadn't spoken since. Her father paced the fire circle, jaw clenched until it bled.

Near the water hut, Jake saw Renn sobbing into his mother's arms. Renn's older brother had gone to collect firewood during the attack and hadn't come home. By the tanning racks, Elder Yasha clutched a woven armband left behind by her grandson. "He was on watch," she whispered. "He would not run."

Whispers moved like sparks through dry grass. "Six are missing. Maybe more." "The young ones... taken." "Dragged into the trees."

Jake stood near the center ring, listening, eyes scanning. He'd spent the day tending the wounded, resetting traps, mending a spear shaft. Nothing mended the hollow look in the villagers' eyes.

Tharik approached, hands stained with dried blood. "They took them," he said. "Didn't kill them all. Just enough to distract."

Jake nodded. "Calculated. Malik wanted our focus on the ridge while his best slipped away through side paths."

"Children. Young warriors. Bargaining chips."

"Or worse."

Elder Muna cut in, voice low. "We can't keep fighting every moon and suffer losses each time. We are strong, but we are not endless."

Others pressed in. "Maybe it's time to leave." "We can't keep our own safe." "If we stay, we lose more."

Jake raised a hand. Some quieted. Some didn't.

"I know it's not enough," he said, raw from shouting. "I know we've held the line—but we're still bleeding." He swallowed. "I think I can find them. The ones who were taken."

Gasps. Elder Kori stepped from shadow, cautious. "You speak with certainty for someone so new."

"Not with certainty," Jake said. "Just offering an option."

He knelt by the fire and opened his satchel. The Bridge pulsed softly—and for a blink, the display threw a clean, sterile string of characters like a *brand mark*, then vanished. Villagers stepped back. Elder Kori didn't.

"They fear the cursed fire," she murmured, "but fire, like time, can be shaped."

Jake nodded. "I adjusted scan parameters. If I can isolate movement trails—the energy left by the attackers—I can track where they took the captives."

"Even beyond the cliff's edge?" Tharik asked, disbelief threaded through.

Jake nodded. "I don't need sight. Just residual patterns—heat, motion—anything the conflict left behind. Anything I can map."

Hanno stepped forward—tall, scarred, calm as old stone. "Our trackers know the land," he said. "We read tracks in clay, broken moss, the angle of a bent fern."

Marek added, "Show us where your trail goes cold. We can take it farther."

Tharik's gaze lifted to the trees—marks left by his father's generation. He crossed his arms, quieting the murmurs.

"Even if we find them," he said, "how do we get them back?"

Jake locked eyes with him. "We don't wait for another raid. We strike first."

Elder Muna scoffed but held her tongue.

Elder Kori stepped closer, placed a hand on Jake's shoulder. Her voice stayed soft—and carried anyway. "Then prepare. Not only to follow—but to return with what is ours."

The scouts began to rally. Warriors whispered plans. Grief didn't vanish, but purpose edged in.

And somewhere beyond the village, in the trees, a lone call lifted—an ululating cry that ended in a wet choke—and every head turned, not sure if it was bird... or something listening.

Chapter 9: Echoes of Home

Evening settled low across the village, the sky a deep wash of violet and smoldering gold. Jake leaned against a weathered stone near the firepit, flames casting a rhythmic glow across his face. Around him, voices murmured—quiet, tired. But Jake's gaze wasn't on the fire. It was turned inward, caught between the crackling present and the pull of a past that refused to let go.

He remembered long nights in Waltham—his room cluttered with soda cans and blinking monitors, cables snaking across the carpet like digital roots. A desk lamp always burned, throwing warped shadows over walls peppered with worn posters and handwritten code. Late nights debugging, the silence broken only by keystrokes and the low hum of machinery.

"This…," he murmured, voice low and gravel-thick. "It reminds me of late nights debugging code. When the world felt… safe because I could control it."

A nearby tribesman glanced up, puzzled, but Jake didn't explain. He wasn't really talking to him. He was talking to the part of himself that still lived in that room—the boy who believed logic could explain the world.

"I thought numbers could fix everything," he whispered. "That if the code was right, everything else would make sense."

His hand tightened around a small stone, smooth and cool against his palm. His father's voice—steady, patient—echoed in memory. Even broken things can teach you something. You just have to keep trying.

The past rushed in like a tide: the kitchen table, the scent of solder, wires and frustration and laughter—connection that always felt too brief.

Then his room again. The clatter of keys. Code racing across a glowing monitor. Hours of solitude. He was "Wizard Jake" to the others, but only because they didn't know how lonely he was. He built firewalls around himself—not just in systems, but in life.

And still—he wasn't always alone. Friends clustered around a laptop, faces lit with excitement. Projects. Games. Laughter. When code became conversation, he belonged.

Across the flame, a child struggled with a knotted rope, brow furrowed. Jake watched him and smiled faintly. That was him once—wrestling wire into meaning, stubborn against confusion. That persistence... it never left.

He stood, brushing dirt from his hands with an ease that had grown over the months. The tribe moved in a gentle, practiced dance—preparing meals, mending tools, exchanging soft words. What once seemed alien now fit into an intricate pattern he'd learned to read.

Jake drifted toward the edge of camp where shadows lengthened beneath the trees. Wood smoke and wild herbs clung to the air—and sweat evaporated before it reached his jaw, leaving salt and grit. Still, the past tugged: lines of code flashing behind his eyelids, the isolation that shaped him, the community he never expected to find.

Every step away from the fire was a step toward integration—a collision of timelines, a search for equilibrium between the boy he was and the man he was trying to become.

His steps carried him to a quiet clearing. A smaller fire kept vigil there too—private, watchful. Amna was waiting.

She looked up as he approached, expression unreadable. "You carry the night in your eyes," she said softly.

Jake hesitated. He could have played it off. Could have hidden again. But not this time.

"I wasn't born here," he said, and the words felt like a door finally opening.

Amna didn't flinch. She simply shifted to make room, letting him sit beside her on the old log. Her fingers tapped a slow rhythm against the wood.

"Different how?"

Jake's throat worked once. "I come from a world that's not like this," he began, clumsy and honest. "Where machines hum constantly and algorithms dictate every move. Speed. Connection. Every question has a coded answer. Every error gets patched."

He paused, glancing at her as if asking permission to keep going.

"We think we can control everything with our technology," he continued, slower now. "But here... every step feels like I'm rewriting what I thought I understood."

Amna listened, gaze steady. Her fingers drummed softly, an unspoken rhythm that met his breath.

"Does that make you feel disconnected from yourself?" she asked.

Jake exhaled. "Maybe. Or maybe I've just never had to listen to myself so closely before."

"You bring your world with you," she said. "But this place—these people—they don't want to erase you. They just ask that you pay attention."

"I'm trying," Jake said.

"I can see that."

Silence settled—inviting, not heavy. A space carved out for truth.

"Sometimes I wonder if I fit at all," Jake confessed. "Like I'm afraid of tainting something untouched by my presence—like everything I touch comes with complications."

"Then approach it with care," Amna said. "Understand what it is before deciding how—or if—it should change."

A small smile tugged at Jake's mouth, genuine and tentative. "You make it sound easy."

"It isn't," she said. "But it's possible."

Their eyes held. Something quiet sparked—recognition, and need.

"I worry I've lost my passion," Jake murmured. "Back home there was always something driving me. Here... I'm scared I'm just getting by."

"Perhaps what you're looking for is already here," Amna said. "Not something new to create—something hidden, waiting for discovery."

She placed her hand over his—reassuring, solid—and her voice firmed. "You adapt well. You learn quickly. Even when unaware—you lead."

Jake turned his hand beneath hers until their fingers intertwined, more sincere than anything he'd said since arriving.

They stayed that way while the fire dwindled, the forest breathing quietly around them as something new took root—unseen, undeniable.

A rustle broke the stillness beyond the clearing. Varun stepped into the firelight, eyes gleaming like polished obsidian. His cloak of animal hide hung damp with night air, but his posture carried the heat of a man ready to burn.

Conversation thinned. Warriors froze. Some elders looked up. Others looked away.

Jake rose, instinct pulling him forward—placing himself subtly between Varun and Amna. They hadn't moved far from the larger gathering—close enough for everyone to see.

He'd noticed it more and more lately: Varun's need to speak loudest, to challenge him at every turn. Jake didn't voice his suspicion—not yet. But Varun's timing, his tone, the sharpened gaze... it felt rehearsed. Calculated.

"You speak boldly now," Varun said, voice lifting just enough to hook the circle. "But we've watched. We've listened. And some of us have not forgotten what it means to protect our way of life."

Jake's spine straightened. Amna's hand slipped from his, but her presence stayed taut at his side.

"I've told no lies," Jake said. Calm—while his eyes tracked Varun's angle, his glances, who nodded back.

"No," Varun said, circling the fire like a wolf sizing prey, "but you've built your place on half-truths. Words none of us knew before you came. Tools that do not belong."

Amna stepped forward. Her voice was clear. "He's shared what he knows. With respect. You twist it into fear."

Varun's gaze snapped to her. "And you defend him?" Scorn thickened his words. "You—the voice of reason among us—now kneel to a foreign fire?"

Amna held his stare. Unreadable. But something hard lived behind her eyes: she didn't trust Varun—not anymore. Still, she wouldn't accuse him here. Not yet.

Beyond the clearing, the dark shifted—figures drawing closer. Elders. Hunters. Healers. Faces lit by torchlight and curiosity.

Jake stepped closer to the flame. "I never asked to lead. I only asked to help."

"And in doing so," Varun snapped, "you've weakened us. You've turned heads. Made them question the ways that kept us alive since before your people carved stone."

"I've offered new ways," Jake said, steady. "Not to replace yours—to protect them."

Varun's voice dropped. "You can't protect what you don't understand."

"Then I'll learn," Jake said. "I am learning. That's more than fear ever taught anyone."

Varun advanced a step. "This tribe does not need your learning. It needs loyalty."

Amna moved between them, shoulders square. "And loyalty begins with listening," she said. "Which you stopped doing long ago."

The fire popped. The crowd breathed as one.

Then Elder Kori's voice cut through—soft, and carrying like wind through stone. "Let the fire choose what to burn, Varun. Not your fear."

Heads turned. Even Varun hesitated.

Around him, expressions had shifted. Not all were with Jake. Not all stood with Varun either. Doubt lived in the firelight now, flickering—awake.

"This isn't over," Varun said at last, quieter now, bitten at the edges. He turned and slipped into the trees, swallowed by dark.

Jake's breath slowed, though the fire in his chest still burned. He turned to Amna. "You stood with me."

"I saw the truth," she said—quiet, firm. "I don't look away from truth." Her eyes flicked once toward the trees. "But truth hides behind masks. And some wear faces we used to trust."

The crowd scattered. Some nodded as they passed—quick, uncertain acknowledgments. Others kept their eyes down.

The camp didn't choose tonight.

But it listened.

Jake and Amna sat again near the fire. No more words. Not yet.

Above them, stars pricked the sky like the first points on a larger pattern. Below, the ground beneath Jake felt steady for the first time in weeks.

He was a boy between worlds. A tribe on the cusp of change.

And for now, that was enough.

Chapter 10: The Enemy of My Enemy

The fire circle had emptied to dying coals. Jake sat in the ash-light, staring into the ember glow like it could answer him.

Footsteps. Soft. Certain.

Elder Kori entered the circle without a word. Sage and smoke clung to her robes. She sat across from him, staff laid between her knees.

"I thought you were sleeping," Jake said.

"I rest when I'm needed," she replied. Her eyes caught the ember light. "And tonight, the fire remembers too much."

Jake's throat tightened. "You saw it. Varun isn't just challenging me. He's gathering people."

Kori nodded once. "He doesn't question to find truth. He questions to collect followers."

Jake stared into the coals. "It's measured now. Targeted." His voice dropped. "I think he wants more than influence."

"Say it," Kori said.

Jake exhaled. "I think he's working with someone."

Kori didn't flinch. "You're not alone in that thought." She tapped her staff once—quiet, final. "While you were gone, Amna came to me. Varun's patrols were too quiet. He missed gatherings. No explanation."

Jake's stomach knotted. "He left during the last raid."

Kori's gaze stayed steady. "Not to fight. Not to defend. Not to mourn."

Silence stretched between them, taut as a snare line.

"I don't have proof," Jake admitted.

Kori reached into a pouch and placed a smooth, carved bone token in his palm. Old. Worn by hands. "Truth and proof aren't always twins," she said. "But the forest keeps count when people pretend to forget."

Jake closed his fingers around it. "So I watch him."

"You watch who *follows him*," Kori corrected. "And where his feet go when he thinks no one sees."

Jake nodded, heat rising under his ribs. "If I'm right, he's already given Malik more than our defenses."

"Then he declared war while smiling," Kori said softly. "Those are the deadliest."

She stood, joints creaking. "Speak to Amna. She's watching too."

"Will you tell the others?" Jake asked.

"Not yet," Kori said, turning. "You don't name a serpent until it bites."

She paused at the edge of the circle and looked back once. "Be careful, Jake. Some people wear loyalty like a mask."

Then she was gone—staff taps fading into night.

Jake stayed by the coals, feeling the warmth on his skin and the stone of it in his chest.

He couldn't unsee it now.

Left alone in the dim light of the fire, Jake felt warmth against his skin—but beneath it, something harder. Stone.

Kori was right.

If Varun had chosen a side, it wouldn't be visible in daylight.

It would be hidden.

And it would already be moving.

They met under torchlight far from the village—where the fire did not remember, and no elders watched.

Varun moved like a man expecting betrayal—shoulders tight, eyes cutting to every corner where the light failed. He perched on the edge of a worn bench, coiled with urgency. He'd slipped from the village under the guise of scouting the southern ridge—an errand no one questioned.

This wasn't scouting.

"Our plans must align," Varun said, leaning in. His voice was sharp with the certainty that time was running out.

Malik sat opposite him, relaxed in a way that radiated danger. His massive frame stayed half in shadow, one hand resting on the hilt of a curved dagger. He unrolled a worn map, slow and deliberate. Its edges curled like dried leaves.

"They will," Malik said.

Varun tapped the table once. Twice. "You need what I know. Jake's weaknesses. His habits. His blind spots."

Malik watched him without blinking.

Varun's voice dropped. "Inside information. The boy's vulnerabilities. Do you doubt me, Malik?"

Malik's thumb traced the dagger's hilt—more reflex than threat. "No doubts," he said. "Only questions." His gaze stayed on Varun, heavy as stone. "Why now?"

Varun's jaw flexed. "Because every day the village changes around him." He swallowed the word *worship*, and spat out something cleaner. "Because he makes them listen."

Malik said nothing.

"I know the tribe," Varun pressed. "I know what they fear, what they follow, what they forgive. Jake is a wedge. Are you content to wait until he splits them in two?"

A thin smile ghosted across Malik's mouth. "We share an interest. But I must know your motive."

Varun's fingers stilled. His posture tightened. "He stands in my way," he said flatly. "In Elder Kori's way." His eyes burned low. "When he falls, they will look to me for answers. For leadership."

Malik's silence sharpened.

"And Tharik?" Malik asked at last, disdain roughening the name. "He rallies to protect this outsider like a fool."

Varun's mask cracked. "Tharik is loyal to what's already dead," he sneered. "He can't see what's in front of him. I can use that."

Malik tilted his head. "So you claim. Words are cheap."

Varun leaned forward, too eager. "Then act. He's getting stronger."

Malik leaned in just enough for his shadow to swallow Varun's hands. "We strike when it guarantees victory," he said, voice low and patient. "Impatience destroys fools."

Varun's breath hitched. He forced it steady. "Jake must be crushed."

"And after?" Malik asked.

Varun didn't blink. "After, the tribe needs someone to lead."

Malik's gaze went distant, as if he was already watching the village burn. "He will fall," he said. "But remember this, Varun—" His fingers paused on the dagger. "The boy isn't your only enemy."

Varun rose. He tried to leave without looking rushed. He failed.

He vanished into the torchlit dark.

Malik stayed where he was, the map open, the dagger untouched—listening to the quiet the way a hunter listens for breath. He folded the map closed—not of the village, but of the paths leading out of it.

Chapter 11: The Silence of Lies

The sun had just fallen beyond the western ridge, casting the tribal clearing in dim amber. Torches were lit one by one, their flames flickering nervously in the growing dark.

A circle of faces surrounded the central fire. The clearing—usually kept for celebration and counsel—felt stripped bare of warmth. Shadows danced across each face like uncertain ghosts. The air thrummed with unease.

Varun stepped forward, eyes sharp as flint. "You've brought strange ideas that go against our ways—how do we know you're not leading us into a trap?"

He stood tall, feeding the suspicion pulsing through the crowd. Elder Kori's eyes narrowed. Amna tightened her grip on her spear.

Voices rose.

"His ways are dangerous!"

"He'll destroy us!"

Jake met each accusation head-on, jaw tight. The fire before him was nothing compared to the heat of their fear.

Varun stepped deeper into the circle, hands spread in a false gesture of welcome. "This is not the first time visitors have come through the gateway. Always they bring change. Always danger."

He circled Jake, concern too precise to be real. "How could you grasp our customs? Maybe you're here to steal what you can—leaving devastation behind."

"I'm not your enemy," Jake said, steady. "What I've shared can make life better. It doesn't have to change who you are."

Elder Muna's voice cut in. "What if it changes us anyway?"

Murmurs spread.

Amna stepped forward. "And what if we're already being changed—but not by him?" She turned on Varun. "Where were you when the western sentries reported a figure crossing the outer ridge?"

Varun stiffened. Just enough.

"You knew patrols would be light," Jake said. "Just like tonight—when every guard was pulled here."

The murmurs stopped.

"Conspiracy," Varun sneered. "You reach too far."

Elder Kori stepped forward. "Enough. If there's an accusation, say it plainly."

Jake nodded. "He's working with someone outside the village. Someone like Malik."

Gasps rippled. A blade half-drew before another hand stopped it.

Varun scoffed. "Convenient lies."

Amna lifted her spear—not in threat, but witness. "We tracked Malik's scouts near the river bend. Someone showed them the paths."

A voice called, "Could've been anyone."

Another answered, "Only one of us keeps trail maps."

"You think I would betray my home?" Varun snapped.

"I think you already did," Jake said.

The circle rippled again—panic and doubt colliding.

Elder Kori raised both hands. "Quiet."

She turned to Varun. "Have you spoken to Malik?"

A beat.

Another.

Then Varun smiled—tight, bitter. "If I had... would that be worse than what he brings?"

A rustle broke the air.

Too loud for wind.

Then shouting.

Steel on wood.

A scream from the outer huts.

Amna's eyes widened. "No—"

The forest erupted in fire.

The earth shook as torches burst from the trees like falling stars.

This wasn't a raid—it was a strike.

Malik's warriors crashed through the perimeter, war paint glowing like masks of wrath. They cut straight for the circle—where every elder, scout, and defender had been lured.

Malik's voice split the chaos. "Leave none standing."

Jake's stomach dropped. "The guards... were all here."

Amna grabbed his arm. "He used the meeting."

Jake turned. Varun stood frozen, horror widening his eyes.

This wasn't the plan.

Fire roared. A hut ignited. Smoke poured into the clearing.

"Kori!" Jake shouted.

He saw her—standing amid the chaos, unbowed—then two warriors tackled her down.

Jake surged forward. Fire collapsed between them.

Amna dragged him back. "You go now, you die."

Varun stood motionless at the edge of the inferno, guilt gleaming in firelight—then turned and vanished into the dark.

"Coward," Amna spat.

They ran.

Behind them, the village became a furnace.

Jake didn't look back—but he felt it. Every mistake. Every second of trust misplaced.

When they finally collapsed beneath the trees, the sky burned orange behind them.

The village was gone.

All around them, the tribe was breaking.

A woman was dragged, screaming, into the firelight where others were already bound. A young warrior fell, stabbed from behind. A spear flew from the shadows, skidding past Jake's shoulder and clattering into a post.

Malik stepped through the chaos like a phantom king—untouched, unhurried. He moved toward the captives, issuing commands as if sorting tools.

"Take her. That one. That one. Leave the rest. Burn everything."

Jake saw Kori once more—being hauled toward the edge of the village. The chaos blurred as her captors dragged her across trampled earth and shattered debris. Her eyes found his.

Bruised. Blood at her temple. Unbowed.

She was taken past the smoldering remains of the communal fire pit toward an imposing wooden structure already filling with prisoners.

Then she was gone, swallowed by Malik's soldiers.

Jake lunged forward—but Amna caught him. Her grip was iron.

"We can't save her now."

"We can't let them take her!"

"We can't help her if we're dead!"

He faltered. Behind him, fire devoured everything—homes, memory, future. Sweat evaporated before it reached his jaw.

They ran.

The clearing became a furnace. Flames roared. Bodies fell.

Jake didn't look back—but he felt it: every mistake, every moment of blind trust, every second too slow.

They crashed through the underbrush until the sounds of slaughter thinned and vanished. They collapsed beneath a low canopy, lungs tearing at cold air. Behind them, the sky glowed orange, as if the sun itself had bled out. Smoke crept through the forest in slow coils, thick with ash and memory.

Jake lay on the ground, coughing, staring sightlessly into the leaves above.

The village was gone.

Nothing left but the hiss of fire and the echo of screams.

For a time, neither of them spoke.

Jake leaned forward, hands locked around his knees, breath ragged. His palms were scraped raw. A streak of soot marked his cheek like war paint he never chose.

Amna sat against a tree, spear braced beside her, hands clenched on the haft. Blood—not hers—darkened her tunic. Her eyes flicked to Jake, sharp and calculating, but not unkind.

"I should have seen it sooner," Jake said.

Amna said nothing.

"Varun played us. And I let him. I gave him room to speak—to twist—"

"You gave him rope," she said quietly. "He used it to hang the village."

Jake flinched.

Silence returned—heavier now. A silence full of names neither of them spoke.

Then Amna said, low and steady, "Kori knew. I saw it. She chose to stay. She wanted to see what would break."

"She shouldn't have had to," Jake said. His eyes burned—not just from smoke. "We lost everyone. We lost everything."

Amna didn't correct him.

She reached into her pouch and drew out a fragment of blackened wood, its edges still warm. One side bore a crude mark: a spiral carved inside a circle.

"This was nailed to a watch post," she said. "I saw it before we ran."

Jake frowned. "What is it?"

"Malik's mark. Or part of it. He doesn't just take land. He leaves a fracture."

Jake reached out. His fingers brushed the carving—

—and his rig chirruped softly.

A low-frequency pulse passed through the air, barely audible.

They froze.

"What was that?" Amna asked, rising.

Jake unclipped the rig. The interface pulsed once—an irregular spike—then dimmed.

"It's reacting," he said. "To the symbol. Or the wood. Or... something Malik left behind."

"This wasn't a raid," Amna said. "It was a strike."

Jake nodded. "He took more than people." He looked toward the horizon, where smoke still crawled upward. "He disrupted everything."

"Some escaped," Amna said. "Scattered into the forest."

The rage in Jake's chest cooled into focus. "Then we find them. All of them."

He stood. "We don't chase Malik. Not yet. We regroup. We rebuild."

Amna studied him—then nodded once. "There's only one place left he doesn't know."

"The cave," Jake said.

She raised a brow. "You remember it."

"Thalik mentioned it," Jake said. "A place of echoes. Silence. Memory."

"And safety," Amna said. "Beyond the eastern ridge. A day if we move fast."

Jake looked once more toward the ruined village—torches guttering like dying stars.

"Then that's where we lead them."

Amna extended her hand—not urgent. Certain.

Jake took it.

Together they vanished into the forest, threading through smoke and sorrow toward what remained.

Behind them, the clearing burned.

Ahead, the forest deepened.

And somewhere beyond it, the cave waited—silent, ancient, untouched by Malik's fire.

Hours had passed since the attack. The moon hung high and pale, diffused by smoke drifting through the canopy. The air was cold—too cold for the season. The silence pressed in.

They marched single file through twisted roots and uneven ground. The forest felt wrong. Trees leaned unnaturally, bark carved with old marks and talismans. No birds. No insects.

Only the soft scuff of bound feet.

At the center, Elder Kori walked upright despite the bruises across her face and the rope at her wrists. Her eyes tracked the terrain—not for rescue, but for exits.

Around her, the captives moved in exhausted silence. A young warrior dragged one leg, jaw locked against pain. A woman with a long braid kept a child close, murmuring comfort without words. Tharik stumbled beside them, his arm bound tight to his ribs, breath shallow. One guard stayed close—aware that even wounded, Tharik's mind was dangerous.

Malik's warriors surrounded them without taunts or cruelty. This was not conquest.

It was control.

The trees thinned. Torchlight pooled ahead.

Malik waited in the clearing, arms crossed.

"Bring them forward."

They obeyed.

Kori was pushed before him. She did not bow.

"Elder," Malik said, offering a mock nod. "I hoped they'd bring you."

"You hoped for many things tonight," she replied. "Some came true."

His smile thinned. "You speak plainly. Good."

The others were forced to their knees. Kori remained standing.

"You gain nothing from this," she said. "Fire doesn't make a tribe."

"I don't want a tribe," Malik said, circling her. "I want the fracture."

He gestured to the captives. "Already your people doubt the outsider."

"They doubt because of your puppet," Kori said calmly.

"Varun played his role."

"He'll burn with the rest," Kori said. "You built your fire on ash."

Malik shrugged. "Put them in the pit."

No light.

No words.

They were dragged beneath a massive, root-twisted tree. The trapdoor yawned open like a wound. A child whimpered.

Kori met Malik's gaze one last time. "You are not the first to believe pain creates loyalty."

He said nothing.

The trapdoor slammed shut.

Darkness swallowed them.

Inside the pit, breath came loud and fast. Someone sobbed.

Then Kori spoke.

"He will come," she said, steady in the black. "Not to save us—but to end this."

No one answered.

But someone believed her.

Elsewhere in the forest, under a cover of old branches and rustling leaves, Jake trudged forward, leading a struggling group through cold mist and hidden paths.

He had found them at dawn, just as first light filtered through the canopy. The group moved like shadows, shapes barely visible in the gray hush. Only hours had passed since Malik's attack, yet it already felt distant—compressed by shock into something unreal.

A woman led the way, face smeared with soot, an infant bundled silent against her chest. Her eyes never stopped scanning. Beside her, a young boy walked stiffly, one hand pressed to his side, jaw locked against pain.

An elder followed, steady but hollowed, gaze fixed on memories no longer visible in the world around him.

Jake watched them move from shadow to shadow—a living measure of what had been lost, and what still needed saving.

Amna ranged ahead, her silhouette slipping between trees. Dried blood darkened her spear shaft, but her steps were quiet, deliberate.

Over the last three months, Jake had stopped counting days and started measuring survival. The Bridge rested against his chest, its pulse faint—steady, restrained. The forest felt older here. Stones bore faded carvings, spirals softened by time. Thalik had once shown him these marks, calling them *echoes*. Jake understood that now.

They paused by a narrow stream. Jake knelt beside a shivering teen and pressed a damp cloth into his hands.

"We're close," Jake said—not to them, but to himself.

Amna returned with a nod. "Stone markers. Another hour east. Hidden under a rock shelf. Safe."

Jake glanced back. The sky still held a dull red bruise of smoke.

"What if he follows?" someone asked.

"He won't," Jake said. "Not yet. He thinks we're scattered." His hand brushed the rig. "We're not."

They moved on.

Just before dawn, the trees fell away into a shallow basin of stone and moss. A collapsed arch leaned into the earth, half-swallowed by roots. Beneath it, darkness opened—not wide, not hostile.

Waiting.

The cave did not announce itself.

Cool air flowed outward. Smoke thinned. Sound softened.

People slowed without being told.

Inside, the air was dry and still. The stone curved inward, marked with worn spirals and circles—stories pressed into the walls by hands that had come here broken and left breathing.

The echoes of fire did not follow them.

Someone sat and cried without sound. A child slept where they stood. Packs were lowered. Shoulders eased.

Jake stopped just inside the threshold. The Bridge was quiet. For once, it had nothing to say.

"We make our stand here," he said.

Amna nodded once.

Behind them, the survivors began to breathe again—not in hope, not yet, but in relief.

The cave did not promise safety.

It promised endurance.

And for now, that was enough.

Chapter 12: The Long Night

The air was thick with the acrid taste of ash and the metallic tang of iron—burnt blood and smoke braided together in the aftermath of chaos. In the distance, the once-deafening sounds of Malik's war party had thinned to fading murmurs, though their echoes still clung like a ghostly refrain.

Jake was the first to enter the cave, ducking beneath the low stone arch. Inside, the shadows did not recoil. They opened. Cool. Still.

Tharik had mentioned this place once, almost in passing—a concealed hollow beneath the eastern ridge.

"Old roots run deep here," he had said. "If danger ever comes too fast, it's where I'd go."

The words settled now, heavy with truth.

Jake guided the survivors with brisk hand signals and hushed instructions. Every step through the damp passage was fueled by memory—Emma's laughter, her sharp eyes, the way she always saw through his bravado. She was more than family. She was his anchor. The thought of losing that connection drove him forward.

He braced a bleeding youth by the arm, steadied an older man with a firm grip on his shoulder. As the tunnel narrowed, the group compressed, footsteps echoing too loudly as dropped spears clinked against stone.

Then the passage widened.

They spilled into a larger cavern where water dripped from the ceiling in slow, patient beats. Villagers stumbled and collapsed against the walls, soot-streaked and pale. Light filtered through jagged cracks above, breaking into fragments across their faces.

Jake scanned once and pointed toward a high alcove. "Over there. Move."

They obeyed—not panicked now, just spent. Some bound wounds with strips of cloth. Others sat and stared. Breath came ragged.

A young boy looked up at Jake. "They just... appeared," he said, voice shaking.

"They knew we'd be there."

"Where's Tharik?"

"They took him."

"My father stayed behind—"

"Argi, sit," an elder said, his voice wavering but firm.

Fear began to rise, sharp and contagious.

Jake's voice cut clean through it. "Listen."

The cavern stilled. Even Amna paused at the entrance, her spear dark with dried blood.

"We're safe here," Jake said. Not a promise. Something steadier than that.

The noise ebbed. People drew closer together. Order returned in small, deliberate movements as Jake moved among them—binding a wound, guiding someone to sit, steadying hands that shook too hard.

Amna came to his side. "Where is Tharik?"

A voice answered from the shadows, rough with grief. "He stayed. Held them off so we could escape."

Amna's fists tightened. Her eyes burned.

"They won't find us," Jake said, surer than he felt. "Not if we keep quiet. This place is defensible."

She studied him, then nodded once. "They won't surprise us again."

"I know."

He looked at them—bruised, bloodied, frightened. Still here.

"I don't have all the answers," he said. "But if we stay together, we survive."

Something loosened. A breath passed through the cavern. Someone leaned back against the stone and slept where they sat.

A distant sound echoed down the passage they'd come from—a ululating cry that ended in a wet choke. Dust sifted from the ceiling.

"They're coming," someone whispered.

Jake met Amna's eyes. Understanding passed between them.

"Then let's get ready," she said.

"Over there," Jake replied. "Move."

They did.

Hours later, the cave held only breath and drip.

Jake crouched by the wall, dragging the charred end of a branch across damp stone. Ash marked a map—circles, angles, exits. Crude. Functional.

He had never mapped a war before. But he knew how to break chaos into steps.

Around him, survivors watched in silence—some upright, some wrapped in blood-stiff cloth. Hands tightened on spears and stones. No one spoke.

"We strike at dawn," Jake said.

Murmurs answered.

"We're not ready," he continued, letting the truth land. "But they think we're finished. That's our advantage."

He marked two clefts in the stone. "Here. And here."

A woman who had doubted him earlier nodded. "We move fast. We get Tharik back."

Resolve spread.

"For Tharik."

"I'm in."

A young woman stepped forward, gripping a jagged bone spear. "I know where they're holding the hostages. My father is there."

That settled it.

People moved quietly, scavenging stones, fashioning slings, memorizing the ash-lines with their fingers. Jake watched them—not with pride, but with the weight of responsibility settling fully onto his shoulders. Sweat evaporated before it reached his jaw.

Amna stood beside him. "It'll work."

"It has to."

She raised her voice just enough. "They don't know who they took."

Fear thinned. Purpose replaced it.

Before dawn, the cave fell still again.

Not silence—poise.

Stone rose around them in layered history: columns worn smooth, walls streaked green and rust-red. Ancient carvings spiraled across the back wall—figures, symbols, time pressed into rock. One mark repeated: a double-ringed spiral crossed by a jagged line.

Jake stood at the threshold between firelight and morning. The Bridge rested quiet against his chest.

Amna joined him. "You haven't slept."

"Didn't need to."

"You're thinking about her."

He pulled the stone disc from his pouch. Smooth. Warm. Alive in his palm.

"It has her signature," he said. "She left it for me. A marker."

"She knew you'd come."

"Or that I'd need to."

He swallowed. "I think she wanted me to finish something."

Amna rested a hand on his arm. "You don't carry this alone."

"It feels like I do."

"You gave us direction," she said. "That matters."

Jake tucked the necklace away and met her gaze. "Whatever happens—we get them back."

"We will."

Behind them, the survivors stirred. Weapons were checked. Breath steadied.

Outside, dawn finally broke.

The cave did not promise victory.

It offered time.

And that was enough.

Chapter 13: Dawn of War

The southern wind bit cold against Jake's skin, but he barely noticed. His gaze was locked on Malik's compound below—a patchwork of stolen order and looming threat, stitched into the narrow ravine like scar tissue across sacred ground.

The camp had grown since Jake last scouted it. What once resembled a scavenger's hideout had hardened into a fortified settlement. Crude walls of stacked stone, reinforced with spears, jutted outward like broken teeth, enclosing a network of huts, longhouses, and fenced livestock pens. Two watchtowers—recently raised—stood crooked but functional, their oil torches burning steadily. Guards posted in pairs scanned the forest with hollow discipline.

Inside the walls, movement never ceased. Dozens of Malik's warriors patrolled in mismatched armor—scavenged plates, bone, bark—many bearing Malik's mark burned into leather bands: a spiral carved within a jagged circle, scorched into wood and cloth alike.

Near the central hearth, children huddled together, wide-eyed and silent, overseen by unarmored women who moved with the taut care of those long accustomed to being watched. These were the unwill-ing—taken from raided villages, forced into service or compliance under threat. Some carried baskets. Others swept walkways beneath an enforcer's glare.

Beyond them moved the willing few—those who had pledged themselves to Malik's vision. Converted, not coerced. Disillusioned warriors drawn by power, purpose, or revenge. Their eyes were hard, their hands never far from a weapon.

Animal pens lined the southern edge—mostly wild boar, half-tamed and aggressive, tusks capped in iron. Near the clearing's edge, a tethered hawk twisted restlessly on its perch, one of Malik's messengers. It loosed a sharp, shrill cry that echoed once off the ravine walls, then cut short, like a warning swallowed.

Smoke drifted from the main longhouse where Malik held court, flanked by his inner circle. Fires burned in shallow pits ringed with obsidian—half ritual, half spectacle. Several elders from conquered tribes sat nearby, heads bowed, their presence symbolic rather than voluntary. Power here wasn't earned. It was displayed. Fear, curated.

Jake studied it all in silence.

From the ridge, Malik's stronghold stretched before them—alive, dangerous, and pretending permanence.

Amna crouched beside him. "They've added sentries since yester-day."

"I see them," Jake murmured, marking rotations on the slate with charcoal. "Twenty-minute intervals. Southern flank's fortified, but the east—"

"—is sloppier," Amna finished. "They don't expect anyone stupid enough to scale that ravine at night."

Jake gave a dry smile. "Lucky for us, stupid is our specialty."

Elder Muna approached, her silhouette pale against starlight. The fire in her eyes hadn't dimmed since the village fell.

"Jake," she said softly. "Are you certain this is the right night? Some think we should wait. Heal more. Scout longer."

Jake knelt to face her, ash smudged across his hands, slate clenched tight. "If we wait, they'll move the prisoners. Kori won't survive another interrogation. And if they break Tharik…" He exhaled. "Malik will know everything."

Amna didn't look away from the compound. "We lost the village. We're not losing our shaman—or our strongest fighter."

Muna studied them, then nodded once. "Then it's tonight. No fires. No blood unless forced. Women and children untouched."

"That's the line," Jake said.

They moved into formation, teams falling into roles mapped over two nights: one to guard the caves, three to strike—diversion, rescue, retrieval.

A scout emerged from the brush, breath fast but steady. "Confirmed. Tharik's alive. Separate holding pit on the north side, beyond the outer fields. Near the livestock."

Jake's jaw tightened. "Then we start there."

They descended, the world narrowing to shadow and movement. Rain-soft earth swallowed their steps. Trees thinned as Malik's perimeter loomed.

Jake stopped beneath a fire-scarred, leafless tree and checked the rope at his shoulder.

Amna whispered, "The pit's ahead—see the broken wagon?"

He did. Sunken ground. A crude metal grate weighted with stones, bound tight with cord. A torch burned nearby, abandoned by a guard distracted by smoke and shouting.

Jake raised a fist. Silence.

They crept forward. From the pit came a low, broken groan.

"Tharik?" Jake whispered.

No answer.

Then a shape shifted upward—one eye swollen shut, face bloodied and smeared with dirt.

"You took your time," Tharik rasped.

Jake grinned. "Had to keep the welcome party entertained."

He cut the cord with a flint chisel. The bindings snapped.

"Can you walk?"

"I'll crawl," Tharik said, hauling himself upright. "They worked me over for two days."

"Not finished yet," Jake said, steadying him as smoke bloomed near the compound gate. A high whistle split the dark. Shouts followed.

The distraction had begun.

Tharik turned toward the noise. "You bring the whole tribe?"

"Only the ones who won't break," Amna said.

He huffed—half laugh, half pain. "And after this?"

Jake's eyes hardened. "Then we disappear before Malik understands what he lost."

With Tharik leaning on Jake's shoulder, they slipped back into the dark—shadows within shadows—one step closer to the heart of the stronghold.

The eastern wall of Malik's compound loomed ahead—a jagged patchwork of stone, dried mud, and scavenged timber, its base sloping into a narrow ledge carved by ancient erosion. Above, sharpened stakes jutted outward like a predator's teeth, but the natural overhang beneath offered just enough concealment to move unseen.

Jake led the way, fingers biting into the gritty ledge, each step deliberate. Below, the ravine opened into the rear quarter of the compound, where storage sheds and water basins stood in loose formation—unguarded, forgotten amid the diversion.

Tharik followed, wounded but focused. He limped without complaint, keeping weight off his bad leg, eyes sharp despite the bruising.

They slipped through a narrow breach in the lower wall—half-collapsed stone, once reinforced, now loosened by storm and neglect. Smoke from the diversion thickened around them, curling over rooftops, cloaking their movement like a second skin.

Inside, Malik's village pulsed with confusion. Guards sprinted toward the gates, shouting over one another. Smoke bombs hissed and billowed in unnatural purples, yellows, and pale green—concoctions Jake had prepared days earlier from crushed berries, powdered roots, and fire-seed oil.

From a high wooden platform above the command hall, Malik's voice cut through the chaos with lethal calm.

"Seal the eastern side—circle back on the far flank! No one gets out!"

Jake ducked behind a leaning structure of woven reeds and clay. Amna pressed in beside him, pointing.

"There." She indicated the largest building—the command hall. "Main entrance. Two guards."

Both shouted orders into the chaos, spears raised, backs straight. Distracted—but disciplined.

Jake scanned once more.

To the right, half-hidden by stacked baskets and a collapsed shelter, a side entrance yawned—a low stone-framed door, barely ajar.

"There," he whispered.

They moved as shadows, sliding between walls, ducking beneath a torn canopy. At the door, Amna checked the hinge and slipped inside first, blade drawn.

The air hit hard—oppressive, hot, heavy with smoldering herbs and old blood. Sweat evaporated before it reached Jake's jaw. Woven mats lined the walls; the stone floor beneath their boots was worn smooth by years of ritual and gathering.

At the hall's center, bound to a column carved with ancient glyphs, sat Elder Kori. Her silver hair was matted with blood and ash, but she sat upright—regal even in chains. A dim brazier cast shifting amber and black across her face.

Jake dropped to one knee.

"Kori."

Her eyes opened—calm, deliberate. "You came."

"I said I would."

A ghost of a smile touched her mouth. "I saw it in the fire. You'd find me here."

Amna swept the room. "We don't have long."

"Not yet," Kori said quietly. "There are more. Back rooms—fifteen, maybe twenty. Most tied. A few unconscious. One barely breathing."

Jake's jaw tightened. "Tharik, can you move her?"

Tharik stepped in, leaning on a broken spear shaft. "Try to stop me."

Jake pressed a cloth-wrapped stone into his hand. "Flash trap. Wick's short. Toss it if things turn."

Tharik took it without question. "I'll leave them a message."

Jake nodded, then turned to Amna. "Finish it."

They split. Jake rigged the main corridor—wedging a brittle support beneath a floor slat, threading vine to a trigger plate. If stepped on, the hallway would drop into the trench they'd dug and camouflaged during scouting.

Amna vanished into the rear chambers. She returned moments later, eyes fierce.

"Found them. Rawhide bindings. Two children. One elder barely breathing. Patrol incoming—two, maybe three."

"Quiet," Jake said.

The first guard rounded the corner with a sneer—Amna's dart struck his neck. He fell without a sound.

Jake surged forward, blade flashing. With Savi, he cut bindings fast, urging captives upright. A woman—Sola, the healer—clutched his arm.

"Kori?"

"Safe. Head for the breach. Tharik's waiting."

A whisper from the shadows. "My son—"

Jake turned. A boy no more than ten crouched against the wall, eyes wide. Jake lifted him gently. "With me. You're both getting out."

Shouts rose outside. The smoke thinned. Time was bleeding away.

Jake hoisted the boy and signaled retreat.

At the breach, Tharik waited, Kori braced against him as he shepherded survivors into brush cover. Relief flickered across his face as the last captives emerged.

Jake passed the boy off and Amna caught his arm. "What are you doing?"

Jake's gaze snapped to the watchtower, urgency coiling tight in his chest. "The rig. I buried it there before the raid—split in pieces. If Malik finds it..."

Amna didn't hesitate. "You have one minute."

Jake nodded once and ran—vanishing into smoke and shadow as the compound roared behind him.

By the time Jake reached the ridge, the compound behind him had erupted into chaos. Malik's voice thundered across the ravine like a storm given form, issuing commands sharp enough to cut through the last wisps of smoke. The flash trap had detonated. The guards had found the empty hall. But they were too late.

Jake skidded to a halt beneath a blackened tree scarred by lightning, its bark split and hollowed. He dropped to one knee, fingers clawing at damp soil. Sweat evaporated before it reached his jaw. His heart pounded—not from fear, but urgency.

He found it.

A strip of leather. A buried satchel. The familiar weight of his portable rig, hidden days earlier beneath stone and brush. He yanked it free, brushing dirt aside. The leather was damp, but intact.

No time to check the screen.

He turned and ran.

When he crested the final ridge, the trees opened like parting curtains. Below, in the shadow of the cliffs, the cave mouth flickered with torchlight and the pale wash of dawn. The wind shifted. Jake caught moss, damp stone—and the smoke from fires that had once devoured their village.

Then he saw them.

Survivors. Children. Elders. Warriors bruised and bloodied, but standing.

They poured from the cave, blinking as if the world had returned too quickly. The rescue team emerged from the tree line—Kori leaning on Tharik's shoulder, Amna steadying a limping villager, Savi guiding the children forward one by one.

For a heartbeat, the world held.

Then it broke open.

A boy sprinted, crying out—his ululating cry ending in a wet choke as he collided with his mother. An elder dropped to his knees, weeping without sound. A wounded scout, carried by two others, barked a ragged laugh and raised a fist to the sky.

They were home.

Amna helped Kori onto the stone path. Kori lifted her hand—not high, but steady. Her voice carried through the dawn, rough but unbroken.

"The fire took our walls," she said. "But not our roots. We are not broken. We are reforged."

Silence—then a cheer. Small at first, swelling as if a breath long held had finally been released. It rolled across the gathering, a drumbeat of life.

Jake stood at the clearing's edge, the satchel tight in his arms, breath caught in his throat.

For the first time, it felt real.

Not just survival.

Not just escape.

Belonging.

Later, as night returned to wrap the cave in silence, they gathered in what had once been a winter shelter—now claimed as the Stone Hall, a space for leaders, decisions, and renewal. The central fire pit burned low, its embers breathing softly, casting flickering shadows across carved walls layered with smoke and ancient soot.

Jake sat cross-legged, The Bridge beside him. Amna sat to his left; Tharik leaned beside her, a bandage pressed tight to his ribs. Kori and Muna sat across the circle, flanked by warriors and scouts who had proven themselves in the raid.

Tharik spoke first. "They were preparing to move the prisoners. Malik thinks we retreated far west. He didn't expect us to strike this soon."

"He will now," Jake said. "And he won't make the same mistake again."

Kori's eyes gleamed in the firelight. Weariness lined her face, but her spine was straight. "He fears you, Jake. Not because you're a warrior—but because you think differently. You bring tools and ideas he can't control."

Jake shifted, suddenly aware of every gaze. "It's just strategy. Logic."

Amna smirked. "And bombs made from fish bladders and fermented berry juice."

Tharik chuckled, then hissed through his teeth. "And don't forget the tripwire. That guard nearly danced."

The fire popped—sharp, sudden—sending sparks up the stone throat of the hall.

Kori didn't smile. "You offer more than tactics. You've given us new ways to see the old world. That terrifies him."

Jake reached for the satchel. He unbuckled the flap and drew out the rig. Its screen glowed softly—then pulsed.

Once.

Again.

Subtle. Repeating. And not his doing.

Jake frowned. "That shouldn't be active. I shut the beacon off after the last scan."

Amna leaned closer. "What is it?"

"Feedback." He tapped the display. A waveform shimmered, uneven. "Something's out there—broadcasting. Or... resonating."

Tharik's brow furrowed. "You think it's Emma?"

Jake hesitated. "I think something from my time—or someone—is reaching across the fracture. And my Bridge is listening."

Kori's voice was quiet, carrying the weight of old truths. "The past echoes. Sometimes so loudly it breaks the walls between."

Jake lifted his gaze, resolve settling in. "If I can trace the source of these disruptions, we might learn who—or what—is causing the storms and the glitches. And maybe find a way to stop them."

Kori placed her hand on his shoulder, warm and steady. "Then we stand with you. Not because you came from another time—"

She met his eyes.

"—but because you belong to this one now."

The cave had gone quiet—not with fear, but with exhaustion giving way to reflection, with hearts finally allowed to rest.

Jake sat alone near the mouth of the alcove, his silhouette backlit by the faint silver wash of early dawn. The stone beneath him was cool, worn smooth by time and water. Beyond the jagged opening, the sky shifted—black softening to slate blue, then to the faintest blush of gold.

Behind him, the last coals whispered in their cradle of stone. A single ember cracked—sharp, dry—then fell silent. Smoke curled lazily upward, thinning into the ancient breath of the cave.

A soft footstep sounded behind him—measured, light. Jake didn't turn. He knew the rhythm of Amna's approach now.

"You haven't slept," she said.

He shook his head, eyes fixed on the changing sky. "Didn't feel like it."

She lowered herself beside him, draping a worn fur across her shoulders. Their arms brushed. The contact was small, grounding. Sweat from the long night had dried on his skin so completely it felt tight, as if it had evaporated before it reached his jaw.

"You're thinking about her again," Amna said gently.

He didn't ask how she knew.

Jake reached into the inner pouch of his satchel and drew out the stone disc necklace—the one Amna had given him days ago beneath the cave, her expression solemn. The disc rested cool and smooth in his palm, pristine, as if untouched by the centuries it must have crossed.

"It's strange," he murmured, turning it slowly. "When you first gave this to me, I didn't think much of it. Just another relic. But the first time I really scanned it—something hit me."

Amna watched his face, saying nothing.

Jake traced the spiral grooves with his thumb. "It isn't just ancient. There's structure in it. A resonance pattern. My Bridge picked it up." He swallowed. "And it wasn't random."

He looked at her. "It was her. Emma. Her signature. The same code she used when we built together—buried in the frequency like a fingerprint."

Amna frowned. "But you said she never gave it to you."

"She didn't," Jake said. "She bought one like this years ago. Flea market junk, she called it. Wore it under her hoodie all the time." A faint, pained smile. "I forgot she even had it."

"And now it's here," Amna said softly.

Jake nodded. "You said your father passed it to you."

"He did." Amna looked down at the disc. "He said it came from a traveler. A girl with strange eyes who vanished into the woods before I was born. She gave it to the tribe as a warning. My father kept it. Thought it was sacred."

Jake stared at the stone. The spirals seemed to shift in the dying firelight. "I don't know if it was my Emma. Or another version. Another fracture." His voice tightened. "But if it's her..."

He stopped.

Amna leaned closer. "Then she came back for a reason."

Jake nodded once. "Maybe not to be saved." A breath. "Maybe to save us."

"What happens next," Amna said, "isn't just your burden. You gave us direction. You gave me that, too."

He turned to her. "I never meant to lead anyone. I was just trying to find her."

"Maybe leading us is how you find her."

Their eyes met—not with tension, but with something quieter. Steadier.

From deeper in the cave, life stirred—low voices, the scrape of stone, a child's sleepy cough. The others were waking.

Jake tucked the necklace away, rose, and faced the light breaking over the ridge.

"Whatever happens," he said, "we get them ready."

Amna stood beside him. "We will."

The sun crested the ridge, spilling light across a landscape still scarred by fire. Under the gold-tinged sky, movement returned.

Jake stood on the overlook with Amna at his side and Tharik on the other. Behind them, villagers emerged from the cave. Children carried tools. Warriors carried stone-tipped spears. Elders gathered in small knots, speaking quietly, purpose in their voices.

They weren't hiding anymore.

Kori stepped forward, her robes crudely mended, her posture unbroken. She raised a hand to the dawn.

"We have lost our home," she said, voice clear, "but not our way. The fire that burned our walls lit the path we must walk. We are not broken. We are reforged."

A cheer rose—low at first, then steadier, stronger.

Jake felt it settle into his chest like a drumbeat.

Not just survival.

A beginning.

Chapter 14: Time's Cruel Hand

Hidden from view, the cave lay behind a thick curtain of vines and rough rock, its mouth swallowed by shadow. The path leading to it was a narrow, winding trail lined with tall ferns and dense underbrush, known only to locals. As dusk settled, shadows lengthened, obscuring the entrance. Two guards stood watch at the cave's mouth, their shapes barely discernible against the stone.

Inside, the air was cool and damp. Water dripped steadily, the sound matching the low murmurs of villagers huddled together. Flickering torches cast an unsteady light across walls carved with ancient symbols that seemed to shift as the flames wavered. The atmosphere was tense but not hollow—a refuge carved from stone where fear pressed close to hope.

"The caves will hold," one man murmured. "Like a crab's shell through a storm."

"And if they crack?" a woman shot back, hands shaking around her spear. "Then we die buried. Like the lost."

Children clung to their mothers, wide-eyed and silent. The injured lay in neat rows, bandages dark with blood and sweat. An older woman knelt near the wall, brushing dust from a broken carving—perhaps her husband's, or her son's. Her hands stayed steady even as her breath hitched.

Every movement carried the weight of an uncertain future.

Apart from them, Jake crouched beside his rig. The device glowed faintly, casting a green halo over his fingers. The casing was scorched, the screen cracked at one corner. Still, it worked. Still, it hummed.

Jake moved along the edge of the firelight, feeling the tension coil around him. Some met his eyes with gratitude; others turned away, their expressions tight with suspicion. He caught fragments of whispered conversation—outsider, disruption—words tossed like stones.

He understood. He'd taught them stronger shelters, better preservation. But to some, he was still an intrusion. Technology felt dangerous to them, a signal flare to enemy tribes. Jake could respect that caution. He represented change, and change came unevenly.

In his hand, he turned Emma's stone disc necklace. He remembered teasing her about it—Did you raid a costume shop for this bling?—and her grin as she shot back, You just don't get style.

The memory tightened his chest.

The disc pulsed faintly now, warm against his skin. Not heat—sweat had dried on his neck before it reached his jaw—but something deeper. Resonance. Like the portal's hum, distant but insistent.

Jake glanced toward the camp as the murmurs softened, one by one. Silence edged closer. The weight on his shoulders wasn't just The Bridge—it was responsibility.

He took a breath and shifted the strap. The caves held secrets and possibility: a place to learn, to merge old knowledge with new ways. Each step forward felt deliberate.

The pulses faded. Jake slung The Bridge higher and moved with the others.

"The boy should stay behind!" someone shouted.

"He moves like a shadow," another said. "And shadows bring destruction."

"He fights for us," a gruff voice countered—a man missing two fingers, shawl stiff with blood. "Malik struck first. The boy struck back."

"But look what follows him," a woman snapped. "Even the sky breaks. Even time bites its own tail."

Their stares pressed in. Jake swallowed the heat rising in his chest. He wanted to shout—I didn't ask for this—but guilt was louder.

Because part of him had wanted it. To test The Bridge. To understand the anomaly.

He hadn't fallen into chaos. He'd gone looking for answers inside it.

Amna met his gaze. A single nod. Quiet. Unshaken—like stone that remembers change.

The cave entrance loomed ahead, dark and jagged like a forgotten beast's mouth. Inside, the tribe regrouped. Bodies—living and wounded—clustered near torchlight. Fear lingered in the damp air.

"Can we fight again?" a boy whispered.

"We must move before dawn," an older woman said. "These caves have no roots."

Hide tents fluttered in drafts. People wrapped themselves in thin blankets and thinner hope.

An elder stepped forward, eyes sharp. "We've faced cold before. Lost our strong. But we are not hollow. Not yet. If the cave holds, so do we."

His words settled like an old chant.

The hush broke.

"Attack... the tear in time... the burning sky," someone whispered.

A mother tightened her grip on her child and looked straight at Jake. "Why now?" she asked. "Why this boy?"

Jake stayed silent. He couldn't give them the truth—that he feared the chaos might be tied to him. To his arrival. To the portal's glow and hum.

Varun was dead. The elders would read signs and dreams, but none could read time the way Jake could—or should have.

Amna stepped forward. "There is change," she said, voice steady. "But not destruction. Not yet. We stand because we know how to rebuild."

She met their eyes one by one.

"The sky cracked before," she said. "And we buried our dead then, too. Yet here we are."

Some nodded. Some didn't.

"More spears," someone muttered.

"More answers," Jake said quietly.

He gripped The Bridge. It pulsed—once—like a heartbeat stumbling. Static whispered. He followed it deeper into the cave, away from firelight, away from accusation.

Behind him, voices rose again.

"The boy will not save us."

He didn't turn back.

The Bridge powered up. Green light washed his face. Data jittered across the screen.

SYSTEM BOOT... STANDBY

READING TEMPORAL INTEGRITY...

[WARNING] PORTAL_COHERENCE_LEVEL: 12%

Time threads scattered like broken code.

"It's not just breaking," Jake whispered. "It's bleeding."

Then he saw it.

Buried in the noise—patterns that weren't his.

His stomach dropped.

It wasn't just the rift.

Something else was here.

Behind him, voices erupted—anger, fear, prophecy. A single sound cut through it all: a ululating cry that ended in a wet choke, silenced too fast.

Jake turned back, lifting The Bridge.

"The portal affects everything," he said. "And something's disrupting it. Something that doesn't belong here."

"It wasn't broken until you arrived," a girl snapped.

"Malik hunts with blades," a man said. "But this—this has no shape."

"If I hadn't come," Jake shot back, voice raw, "you'd still be running. Or dead."

The elder spoke again. "By dawn, the mountain's protection fades."

Jake nodded once. "Then dawn is all I need."

The glow sharpened his face—fatigue, resolve, etched together. He tightened the strap.

Amna stepped beside him, half in light, half in shadow.

"Can you stop the timeline from falling apart?"

Jake met her eyes. "I have to."

She didn't comfort him. She believed him.

"Then move," she said. "The future won't wait."

Time stretched and splintered.

The cave held its breath.

Jake crouched near the rear wall, the device glowing against the dark. Light and data danced across the screen in chaotic bursts—signatures blurring, too fast, too erratic. It was like watching reality collapse in real time.

The torch beside him fluttered—then froze, flame suspended mid-flicker before snapping back with a faint static crack. Dust rose and fell in stutters, like a video buffering.

Farther off, footsteps echoed—then echoed again, a beat too late. Reality replaying itself badly.

The tribe was leaving.

"They don't believe in you, Jake," a voice said.

Amna's? A memory? Both?

The cave repeated the words, a second whisper lingering after the first like a shadow of sound.

And what do you believe?

Jake closed his eyes and forced his breathing steady. Every pattern on the screen screamed collapse. The Bridge pulsed hotter now, its edges warm beneath his fingers—sweat evaporated before it reached his jaw.

He clutched the necklace. Emma's.

Once just a trinket. Now it pulsed faintly, its rhythm syncing with the rig's strange heartbeat.

Across the far wall, a carving shimmered—briefly becoming something else—then snapping back. The past was trying to overwrite the present.

Jake refocused, fingers flying across the interface. Seconds burned. He logged variables—his presence, the portal, the necklace—cross-referenced event stamps, synced against chrono-degradation curves.

What's causing the unraveling?

Every theory fractured into more questions.

Panic scratched at the edges of his thoughts. He forced it down.

Think.

Focus.

Map the corruption.

Distortions. Discrepancies. Patterns failing to reconcile.

Then—

A torch down the corridor flared backward, its flame reversing for a heartbeat before correcting. Amna passed it, and her shadow lagged behind her—one full step late—before snapping forward to rejoin her feet.

Jake's breath caught.

Not just me.

The realization hit like a pressure drop.

The fracture wasn't singular. There was another cause. Another presence.

The Bridge pinged.

ANOMALY DETECTED: OBJECT_THETA_01

EMMA_NECKLACE: TEMPORAL SIGNATURE MISMATCH

ANOMALY DETECTED: ENTITY_ALPHA_09

SUBJECT JAKE: INTERFERENCE VARIABLE UNSTABLE

Jake's heart stuttered.

Two sources. Two disruptions.

"It's not just me," he whispered. "It never was."

"Then who?"

He startled—too sharp, too late.

Amna stood at the edge of the shadows. Behind her, the torchlight fractured her silhouette into three overlapping shadows, each slightly out of sync.

"Who is it?" she repeated.

Jake turned the screen toward her, throat tight. "I don't know. But the readings—there's another force. A different signature. It doesn't match mine."

Amna stepped closer, studying the shifting waveforms. "You think they'll believe this?"

He let out a humorless breath. "Do you?"

She considered for a heartbeat, the flickering light sketching and resketching her face.

Then she nodded. "It's a start."

Jake turned back to the rig.

The readout pulsed.

So did the timeline.

He'd find the answer.

He had to.

The Bridge chirped softly as he redirected the stabilizer feed, bleeding excess energy into the containment shell. The glow steadied—barely.

SIGNAL LOCK: 73%

Amna leaned in. "That's her."

"Emma's signal," Jake said. "Or what's left of it."

"You're chasing shadows."

"No," he said quietly. "I think she's been trying to reach me."

Behind them, voices called out. Orders. Movement. The tribe withdrawing deeper into the caves. Torches receding one by one.

No one lingered.

Except Amna.

"You've seen too much to stop now," she said.

Jake watched the readings stabilize—still fragile, still wrong. "It's not ready. If I open it now... I don't know what comes through."

"Then don't," Amna said. "Not yet."

She stood beside him—not to pull him away, but to hold the line.

The Bridge cooled slightly, its pulse slowing. Not fixed. Just delayed.

"I bought us time," Jake said.

"Then we use it," she replied. "To plan. To survive."

The last footsteps faded into the stone corridors. Above them, the sky flickered—stars frozen mid-blink, as if unsure which second to exist in.

Jake didn't look away.

He understood now: waiting wasn't weakness.

It was strategy.

And time—whatever it had become—was no longer on anyone's side.

Chapter 15: Race Against Time

Inside the dim cave, thick with smoke, Jake sat on the dirt floor beside the glowing portal. Its light pulsed low, then high, cutting through shadow like a tear in reality. Blues and whites skated across the stone walls, illuminating stacks of supplies and the half-finished diagrams he'd scratched in charcoal at his knees. With each pulse came a hot, unnatural breeze—sweat evaporated before it reached his jaw—stirring dust and setting bundles of herbs and charms swaying. The cave felt like it was holding its breath, struggling to keep its shape as time unraveled around it.

Another pulse struck. A bowl of powdered flint tipped and spilled, ash scattering across Jake's diagram. He didn't look up.

In front of him sat The Bridge—scarred, dented, months of hard use etched into its casing. The screen skipped, buzzed, then steadied, stubbornly alive.

Jake leaned closer, pale green light washing his face. Status readouts crawled across the display:

TEMPORAL RIFT STATUS: UNSTABLE

PHASE VARIANCE: CRITICAL

SIGNAL LOCK: INTERMITTENT

He wiped soot from the screen. "Yeah," he muttered. "I know."

He cracked open a side panel, fingers finding a frayed fiber-optic line bound with protective vines. A static jolt bit him—sharp and bright—but he held on.

"You'll burn out before I do," he said quietly.

The rig chimed, the sound thin and metallic, like a ululating cry that ended in a wet choke.

SYNC ATTEMPTING...

TEMPORAL STABILIZER: MANUAL OVERRIDE RECOM-MENDED

Jake snorted. "Manual override. Of course."

His fingers flew. "Override delta-phase delay. Anchor to three-point-seven nanocycles. Cascade flux bypass. Lock."

Charcoal lines twisted beneath his hands—loops, equations, arrows crossing arrows—as he reorganized the stabilization sequence. The portal resisted, a pressure like live current pushing back against his grip.

Then the pulse shifted.

For the first time in hours, it steadied—syncing with The Bridge.

Jake exhaled, shoulders sagging, shirt soaked. "That's it," he murmured. "Just breathe with me."

Movement rippled inside the portal. Fractured glimpses flashed past: a mountain split by fire, a city suspended in cloud, a child frozen at the edge of a mirror.

Then his own reflection—older, worn, eyes too knowing—stared back.

The rig chirped.

TEMPORAL HARMONICS: STABLE – 64%

FOREIGN SIGNAL DETECTED

LANGUAGE ENCRYPTED: DECRYPTING...

A voice spilled into the cave, distorted, dragged thin across time.

"Jake Walker. You opened the gate too soon."

His heart stopped.

Symbols streamed across the display—organic, nonlinear, nothing like his code. The signal looped, cohered, then faded.

"You're not noise," Jake whispered. "You're talking to me."

He keyed commands fast.

SIGNAL TRACE INITIATED

CROSS-CHECKING TEMPORAL SIGNATURES...

RESULT: TWO PRIMARY VARIABLES DETECTED

OBJECT_THETA_01 [EMMA_NECKLACE] – FOREIGN SIGNATURE

ENTITY_ALPHA_09 [SUBJECT_JAKE] – INSTABILITY SOURCE

The realization landed hard.

"It's not just me," he said. "You've been here longer than I have." He leaned in. "Show me the convergence."

Stone shuddered. The portal dimmed.

Footsteps pounded toward him.

Amna burst into the cavern, breath ragged, spear dark with blood. "We're under siege."

Jake was on his feet. "Malik?"

"They found the trail. Broke the outer defenses. Elders and fighters are pulling back through the eastern tunnels. Tharik's holding the ridge."

Jake looked at The Bridge. Data still scrolled. Decryption incomplete.

"I need more time."

"You don't have it."

The portal flared again, wind surging, its pulse matching his heartbeat.

Jake turned back to the rig, jaw set.

"Then I'll take it."

Malik stood on the edge of the ravine, studying the hidden cave entrance, half-lost behind twisted roots and broken stone. Rain soaked his shoulders, seeping into armor of fur and bone. The storm that had scattered his men had moved on, leaving the air tight and electric. Water ran down his spine and vanished against his skin, heat bleeding off him despite the cold.

His warriors clustered behind him—restless, armed, hardened by hunger and anger.

Malik's gaze shifted to the slope below. The Elders stood their ground, spears braced, expressions carved from resolve. He respected that. He also calculated how quickly they would fall.

Jori approached, quiet as ash. "Three escape tunnels. Two guarded. One trapped. We breach together?"

Malik shook his head. "No. We drive them inward." His eyes stayed on the rock. "We take the portal. Not just the people."

Jori hesitated. "You believe it's real?"

Malik's jaw tightened. "I saw the sky tear." His voice dropped. "Fire twisting where fire doesn't belong."

The storms replayed in his mind—worse each time, mocking him. He didn't need belief.

"I don't need to believe," he said. "I need control."

The glowing device haunted him. Not a gift—an infection. And the boy who carried it. The Wizard. Malik felt it in his bones: every fracture, every storm, every loss traced back to that machine.

Unease crawled through him, sharp and constant. The air itself felt wrong, as if the world were leaning toward collapse. Doubt had no place here. Only reclaiming what had been stolen.

He lifted his obsidian blade—stone born from the mountain where his ancestors fell. Thunder cracked nearby, a short, tearing boom that ended in a wet choke, vibrating through the ravine.

"On my command."

A war horn answered from below.

Battle ignited—cries, bone striking steel, the rhythm of violence. The defenders fell back with intent, funneling attackers into narrow ground. The Elders fought like cornered beasts.

Malik didn't watch.

He turned to the shadow beside him—one of the storm-displaced outsiders, eyes bright with a curiosity Jake would recognize.

"Is he alive?" Malik asked.

The figure nodded.

"Good." Malik smiled, thin and satisfied. "Then we still have a way in."

He stepped forward as the second wave surged.

"And I will be the one who closes it."

The storm swallowed him whole.

Back in the cave, Jake felt The Bridge vibrating with activity. Warnings crowded the screen as its systems strained under mounting pressure.

DECRYPTION: 89%

SIGNAL STABILITY: DROPPING

TEMPORAL FIELD: INFLUX

[WARNING] COLLAPSE THRESHOLD APPROACHING

He rolled up his sleeves, wiping grime from the solar panel just enough to pull a few more microvolts. The device stuttered and emitted a low, teeth-grinding whine, but it held.

A tremor rolled through the cave. Something heavy struck near the entrance. Screams followed—raw, close—then the ululating cry of a man that ended in a wet choke.

Jake didn't look up. If he did, he'd see Amna. Tharik. The Elders. All of them bleeding while he sat with code and hope.

He pressed the necklace to the input plate. The stone flared, sparks skittering across the rig as energy surged.

OBJECT_THETA_01 — SYNC INITIATED

NEURAL MATCH CONFIRMED: SUBJECT_EMMA

SUBROUTINE UNLOCKED

The screen bloomed—pathways branching like roots finding water. Dormant systems woke.

Jake's fingers flew. "New sequence. Anchor to Emma's thread. Track last known timestamp."

Outside, battle roared. Bodies hit stone. Bone cracked on bone. Another shock rattled the chamber, pebbles clattering down. Jake ducked instinctively, cradling The Bridge as sweat evaporated before it reached his jaw.

Guilt burned hotter than fear. They fought. He fixed time.

PARALLEL THREAD IDENTIFIED

TEMPORAL RIFT STABILIZING

SIGNAL LOCK: 97%

FOREIGN SIGNATURE: ACTIVE

EMMA_PROTOCOL: PARTIAL EXECUTION ENABLED

The portal steadied.

Jake exhaled. The anomaly shimmered—held. No tearing. No collapse. Just an eerie calm.

The light softened, shifting to a muted gold that washed the chamber like breath returning.

It's waiting.

The rig buzzed faintly.

STASIS HOLD: 1 MINUTE 12 SECONDS REMAINING

SYSTEM INTEGRITY: VOLATILE

SUBROUTINE ENCRYPTION: PARTIAL

FINAL INSTRUCTION KEY: MISSING

His stomach tightened.

"Emma," he whispered. "What did you hide?"

Images flashed—fractured and fast. A child's silhouette. A forest burning. A metal door set into ancient stone. His own hands—older, bloodied—reaching.

The Bridge pinged.

MESSAGE FRAGMENT DETECTED:

"He won't see the whole picture until he chooses to let go."

Jake stared. "Let go of what?"

The air rippled, like something massive shifting beyond the veil.

"Override manual control. Hold stasis," he snapped. "Just—give me seconds."

Red flooded the screen.

[ERROR] TEMPORAL STABILITY DECREASING

[WARNING] ACTIVE INTERFERENCE DETECTED

[RECOMMENDATION: DISENGAGE AND RETREAT]

"No," Jake hissed. "Not this time."

The rig burned under his hands. Jagged code flickered, begging for the last piece.

Another impact. Stone burst. A scream—closer.

"Jake—!"

The echo fractured.

"Jake—ake—ake—"

Time folding in on itself.

He turned back to the anomaly. Still holding. Barely. Like glass under strain.

"I'm close," he told himself. "I can feel it."

A final line blinked.

[INPUT FINAL KEY: ???]

The countdown began.

04:09...

04:08...

04:07...

Jake stepped back, fists clenched.

He wasn't ready.

The portal surged, light turning wild again—but it didn't break.

Not yet.

Jake bowed his head, breath ragged. He'd delayed the breach. Bought time.

But Malik was coming.

And next time, time itself might not wait.

Chapter 16: The Siege

Jake crouched low, his form blending into the cavern's dimness. He pressed against the cold, jagged stone, each uneven edge biting through his thin tunic. Beyond the cavern mouth, chaos erupted like a living thing. Arrows sliced the heavy air, slamming into the tribe's hastily raised wooden barricades. Each impact sent vibrations skittering through the rock—a grim drumbeat marking the approach of Malik's forces. The battle edged closer, threatening to swallow them whole.

Torchlight jerked behind him, throwing jittering shadows across damp walls. Steel rang and wood splintered outside, punctuated by a single ululating cry that ended in a wet choke. Amid the din, Jake's fingers flew across The Bridge—his compact coding rig, half miracle, half madness. It was his lifeline, an anchor to a future he was trying to keep intact. Sweat evaporated before it reached his jaw. The warped interface projected a shaky live feed: blurred shapes closing on the entrance paths. Malik's forces pressed forward, relentless, a tide that did not recede.

"Hold steady!" Jake barked without looking up. "Watch the eastern corridor!" His voice struck the cave walls, command and plea fused into one. A young lookout echoed the call, fear cracking his voice. Outside, the defenders strained and held—barely—each second a balance on the edge of collapse.

Jake pushed harder. Code streamed past his vision, too fast to track, a lifeline he had to grab with both hands. This wasn't a puzzle anymore. This was survival. The feed updated—another nightmare: hostiles flanking the eastern cliff trail. Immediate. Dire.

"They're breaching the left flank!" someone shouted from deeper in the corridor.

Jake didn't hesitate. "Stabilize—hold together. Two percent increase," he growled at The Bridge, willing it past its limits. "Don't break on me now." The red icon blinked erratically, the portal's pulse unstable. Each flicker tugged at something deeper than stone, like time itself fraying. He kept moving. The countdown hadn't started—but the clock was already ticking.

The portal symbol throbbed. The air buzzed, electric and tight. "One percent. Two," Jake muttered, forcing his hands steady as the strain pulled at the fabric of the world.

Outside, the defenders fought on. Arrows hammered shields. The enemy tightened the noose, but the tribe dug in, endurance stretched to breaking.

A fierce gust tore through the cave mouths, carrying smoke and iron. Torches flared and guttered, flames snapping wild. Wind and war braided together, the storm rising to meet Malik's fury.

And still, Jake coded.

Outside, the storm raged with the fury of a dying god, the elements conspiring with Malik's attack. Wind tore through the cliffside like a spectral warning, flinging cold rain across the beleaguered defenders. Tribal archers loosed arrows from makeshift cover, firing into the advancing dark. Malik's forces surged again, undeterred. Spears and slings rose in grim unison—a swelling tide threatening to overrun everything.

Inside the cave, Jake was driven deeper into the command alcove by pressure and necessity. The stone narrowed around him like a clenched fist. The Bridge lit his path in pulses of blue and green, bathing the walls in cold, alien light. He slid into position as the stabilizers hummed harder. Blood streaked his sleeves—his or someone else's; it didn't matter. Seconds stretched into aching eternities.

A thunderclap split the air—CRACK—and a loose stone slammed down behind him, missing his head by inches. Dust billowed into a choking cloud. Then came a hollow stillness. Only the hum remained.

Jake locked onto the screen. Blips of light skittered across it like lightning trapped in water. The portal was widening—fast. Intensity climbed through the system, and the sense of inevitability tightened his chest.

"Come on... come on," he muttered, fingers flying. "Recalibrate buffer. Reroute flux—skip accuracy. Just give me seconds."

The Bridge hissed in protest. Sparks snapped from an auxiliary coil. Defiance—and warning.

A readout flashed:

SYSTEM ALERT: UNSTABLE CORE DETECTED
RIFT INTEGRITY: 83%

Jake leaned closer. This wasn't just survival anymore. Something else was waking.

A tremor rolled beneath him. The cave answered with a low groan. He glanced down at the necklace—Emma's. It glowed faintly, pulsing in time with The Bridge's heartbeat. Sweat evaporated before it reached his collar.

"This isn't random," he whispered.

The pull was undeniable. Not coincidence—guidance. As if Emma were reaching from another when.

The necklace flared brighter. The portal answered, resonance building between them like a locked rhythm. Jake felt it click into place.

Then the countdown appeared.

Less than four minutes.

Time slammed back into him, each second striking like a drum. He considered recalibration, algorithm tweaks—but knew it wasn't enough. The portal wasn't just a machine anymore. It was calling.

Ideas collided. Possibilities spiraled. Panic clawed in.

Focus.

He dragged a breath in, steadying himself. The necklace was more than an artifact—it was a bond, a thread stretched across time. He let it guide him.

Back to the screen. Back to the work.

Each keystroke landed harder, faster. Pressure and exhilaration fused, driving him forward.

They were running out of time.

And yet—he was close. Close to something dangerous. Something extraordinary.

As the seconds fell away, Jake braced himself for what came next, clinging to the hope that this—this moment—might be enough to change everything.

COUNTDOWN: 00:03:59...

The ominous beep echoed through the cave, rising in tempo with each passing second. Each tone drilled into Jake's skull, tightening the urgency. His eyes locked on The Bridge, pulling in every fragment of the frantic display. It might be his only lifeline—or their final undoing. He didn't know. He couldn't know. He risked it anyway.

TEMPORAL RIFT STATUS: UNSTABLE

The readout pulsed like a heartbeat—too fast, too loud—reminding him how close they were, or how ruinously far.

STABILIZATION: 99%

TIME SYNC IMMINENT

Another tremor slammed through the cave. Dust fell like ash, smearing the blue glow into shadow.

"You're almost there," Jake muttered through clenched teeth. "Hold... just hold..."

The ground shuddered again, the vibration carrying the muffled cries of defenders at the cave mouth. Chaos pressed inward, as if the universe itself were shoving them toward the edge.

Through the narrow stone gap and swirling dust, a limping shape emerged—

Varun.

His torn tunic whipped like a banner of defeat. Blood streaked his face. He looked half-real, a mirage stitched together by pain.

"They've... breached the corridor," he rasped. "Five minutes. Maybe—maybe less."

Jake didn't look up. He couldn't afford to.

"Then I'll take all five."

The portal's pulse deepened. A low hum rolled through Jake's chest—steady, wrong, intimate.

He pulled the stone necklace free and set it over The Bridge's core plate. The system answered instantly, as if waking from sleep.

SOURCE ID MATCH: EM_001

TIMESTAMP ANOMALY CONFIRMED

OVERRIDE PATH AVAILABLE

ACTIVATE? [Y/N]

Jake froze.

This wasn't possible. Everything he thought he understood unraveled at once. Light intensified, reflecting in his eyes—memory and warning braided together.

Then—

Amna burst into the alcove, soaked and breathless. Tharik followed close behind.

"They're pushing hard," Amna said. "You've got to move."

Jake didn't turn. "The portal isn't tearing anymore," he said. "It's forming a bridge."

Tharik's voice cut through the noise, iron-hard. "And what comes across that bridge?"

Jake stared at the necklace, time stretching thin.

"I don't know. But if we don't do this... we all disappear."

He looked up, face washed in pale light. "Get everyone out. Four minutes. I'll hold the rest."

Amna met his gaze, fierce and unyielding.

"Don't do anything stupid."

Jake smiled faintly. The old defiance flickered.

"Bit late for that."

They vanished into the dark.

The Bridge flared white—blinding, absolute.

TEMPORAL RIFT STATUS: UNSTABLE

TIME SYNC PHASE 1 INITIATED

The countdown marched on.

WARNING: STRUCTURAL INSTABILITY DETECTED

COUNTDOWN: 03:37…

Jake adjusted the controls, his heart hammering like a war drum.

Then the scream came.

A countdown echoed in the cave. As the numbers fell, tension tightened in Jake's chest. The necklace pulsed against his skin, its rhythm syncing with his heartbeat. Sweat evaporated before it reached his jaw. The cave hummed, alive with an eerie song that seemed to coil through the air.

Then a scream shattered it.

It came from the east ridge—primal, wrong—a ululating cry that ended in a wet choke. Not from the cave. Not from now.

Jake froze.

Outside, everything changed. The clash of battle cut off mid-motion, replaced by panicked footsteps. A scout staggered into view, soaked and gasping, eyes blown wide.

"They're retreating!" he shouted. "Malik's troops just stopped. Something out there scared them."

Jake turned sharply. "What did they hear?"

"The scream," the scout rasped. "From the trees on the east ridge. They saw something… and ran."

Another warrior stumbled in, dragging a limp figure behind him. "Found him near the ridge."

Jake's stomach dropped.

Varun.

His body flickered, drifting in and out of focus like a corrupted image. His eyes darted, unfixed, before locking briefly on Jake.

Amna rushed to his side. "Get him inside!"

Varun convulsed, breath hitching. "It—touched me—me—me... in the light. I saw—see—saw... her."

Jake knelt. "What did you see?"

Varun's words fractured, looping. "I didn't—mean—to go. Just... watched. Then the ground—moved. I was—wasn't here. And she—she was—"

"Who?" Jake pressed.

Varun's lips trembled. "A girl. In the light. She... she looked like—"

The necklace flared hot against Jake's chest.

"She knew me," Varun whispered. "Said my name—Jake—before I knew—knew it myself..."

His body went slack.

Silence fell.

Jake stood as The Bridge pulsed, a final line burning across the screen:

FINAL WINDOW APPROACHING

The countdown glared back at him.

00:58

Understanding hit hard. The portal wasn't just open—it was absorbing time, folding past and present together. The mission had outgrown them. Every warning, every careful limit, had already been crossed.

Jake grabbed the necklace. Its glow synchronized with The Bridge, wrong but perfect. Fear and awe cinched his lungs. Malik's retreat made sense now. They were standing at the edge of something vast.

The countdown resumed, each second a hammer blow. The portal called to him, a siren hum beneath the stone. In the narrow corridor, silhouettes rushed toward him—Amna, Tharik, others. They knew.

Jake turned back to The Bridge and plunged into the final commands. Each keystroke carried their fate.

OVERRIDE PATH AVAILABLE. ACTIVATE? [Y/N]

He paused. Breathed.

Point of no return.

"Y."

Light detonated—white, total. Memory and intention fused as the cave flooded with color.

OVERRIDE PATH ENGAGED

TEMPORAL RIFT STATUS: CRITICAL

The countdown kept falling.

00:16...

Each tick thudded in his chest. The portal vibrated, swollen with potential. Fragments of the future flashed—lives intersecting, history bending.

00:10...

Jake clenched his fists, drawn toward the widening rift.

00:01...

The universe seemed to exhale.

Air thickened. Memory surged. With a single blink, present and past braided together.

COUNTDOWN: 00:00

Jake didn't move.

Not yet.

But the portal was open.

And the clock had started.

Chapter 17: Shaman's Gambit

In the dim heart of the cavern, flickering torchlight warped the air. Light skated across uneven stone, stretching shadows into long, ominous shapes. Smoke from oil lamps hung low, clinging to the ceiling as if time itself had slowed. The air was thick—burning herbs, damp earth, and a tension so heavy it pressed against the ribs, warning that something irrevocable was unfolding.

Jake stood at the back, arms rigid at his sides, gaze locked on Varun in the shallow pool of firelight. Every movement Varun made echoed too loudly—the scrape of cloth against stone magnified in the hush. The elders sat in a tight semicircle, men and women etched by wisdom and loss. Their ceremonial robes rustled as they shifted. Whispers died. Backs straightened. Eyes narrowed.

Elder Kori sat at the highest point of the circle, heavy wool and fur draped over her shoulders. Her carved staff rested against her arm. A talisman at her throat trembled faintly, answering something in Varun. She had raised him like a son; his struggle pressed against her like a mirror of her own failures.

With effort, Varun rose beneath the central beam where the light converged. His head stayed bowed, shoulders sagging. When he spoke, his voice carried the edge of confession—quiet, raw.

"I have to tell you, Jake. The breach in the void—my mistakes—they tore open time itself."

The words landed like a drumbeat. No one moved. The silence felt violated, as if an old boundary had been crossed. Somewhere behind them, a young listener gasped.

Jake stepped forward, boots crunching softly on gravel. His voice was low, unyielding. "You're saying you caused the collapse? The instability tearing our world apart—that was you?"

Varun met his eyes. They were hollow. Sweat beaded on his brow, glinting like oil in the firelight. His hands shook, fingers nicked with cuts that shimmered faintly.

"I tried to stabilize it," he said. "I thought I could anchor it. A living tether. If I gave enough of myself—"

"You didn't stop anything," Jake snapped. "You fed it. You turned yourself into fuel."

Kori leaned forward, her staff tapping once against stone. Moisture gathered in her eyes, but her voice held. "Why, Varun?" she asked gently. "You knew the Ancient Ways. I taught them to you. You swore to keep the balance."

Varun turned to her, shame bowing his spine. "I wanted to fix the past. I thought if I blended the old ways with my essence, I could contain it."

Kori closed her eyes. Her breath shook. "And instead, you doomed it to grow with every heartbeat."

Jake stepped between them. "You should have told me. From the start."

"If I had," Varun said, voice breaking, "you would have tried to save me."

"Damn right I would have," Jake shot back. "And maybe you wouldn't be bleeding across timelines."

Silence returned—thick, suffocating. The torches flared, light buckling under the strain.

Varun's knees gave out. He collapsed onto the stone, gasping. His hands pressed into the dirt, smeared with sweat—and something faintly luminous.

"I can't hold it," he whispered. "I'm coming apart. Piece by piece."

Jake knelt, hands hovering, helpless. Varun gripped his forearm, weak but urgent. "The pulse," he breathed. "There's a pattern. I couldn't see it. But you might."

Then he went still.

Firelight glossed his unmoving body. The cavern bowed into silence. Even the torches seemed to lower.

Jake rose slowly, brushing dirt from his knees. His face hardened into resolve. He met Kori's eyes. Grief and understanding passed between them—an unspoken fracture.

Kori looked down at Varun. When she stood, it was with effort. "He was not only my student," she said. "He was our future. And now... he is our consequence."

The words rippled through the crowd. Murmurs spread—raw, uncertain. Young warriors froze, unsure whether to weep or stand. Elders swayed, eyes shut, summoning strength. A low chant began—a mourning song for imbalance, for a wound left open.

The sound filled the cavern, heavy and wrong.

Jake watched the flames flicker against his rig, their light reacting to an unseen pressure beyond sight.

"We don't have time to mourn," he said, voice carrying. "But we will honor him—by fixing what he broke."

Something steadied in the room.

He turned to Kori. After a long moment, she nodded. "Then let his final act be a warning."

Outside, wind surged through the cracks, howling like a living thing. Inside, ancient fire held.

Jake felt the moment harden inside him. "We'll find the pattern," he said. "This isn't over."

Kori's face softened—just briefly—before resolve reclaimed it. "Be swift," she said. "Do not fail."

In the far reaches of the cavern, a young woman began to cry. Her sob cut through the chant like a blade.

The wind battered the stone.

The torches steadied.

And in that fragile light, the fight for the future had already begun.

The cavern remained steeped in a heavy silence, as if the air itself mourned. Time had passed since Varun's death, yet the weight of his absence still pressed on the room. Torchlight wavered along the walls, shadows stretching and recoiling like specters over Varun's still form. Smoke curled toward the beams, and no one dared move.

Jake stepped into the center of the circle. His jaw was set, his voice tightly leashed.

"We don't have any more time."

A low murmur rippled through the elders.

Jake's gaze swept their faces—weathered by loss and ritual. Some met his eyes. Others looked away. Only Elder Kori held his stare, standing beside Varun's body, one gnarled hand resting on the fallen apprentice's shoulder.

"Varun wasn't working alone," Jake said. "This wasn't just a misguided ritual. Malik was involved. He coordinated it."

Gasps and angry whispers followed.

"That's a grave claim," Elder Harun rumbled. "Malik is a warlord of steel and blood. What would he want with our rites?"

"The same thing he's always wanted," Jake said. "Control. He doesn't need to understand the rift—he just needs someone willing to break the locks."

He unclipped the rig from his belt and turned the cracked screen toward them. It pulsed faintly.

"The signal's changed. The energy's irregular. Someone else is tampering with the rift—from the other side."

"Malik," a junior scribe whispered.

Jake nodded. "He bound the rift to Varun's life. Now that Varun's gone, it's destabilizing—and Malik's ready to move."

"And do what?" Elder Nahi snapped. "Reshape the past? Steal the future?"

"No," Jake said evenly. "That's just Malik."

The chamber tightened. A cold wind threaded through the walls, carrying a low moan that set the torches guttering.

"You can feel it," Jake went on. "Time stutters. The sky shifts too fast. Some of you are dreaming things that haven't happened yet."

Silence answered him.

Elder Kori finally spoke. "You speak truth. But crossing Malik's land is no small thing."

"I'm not asking for a war party," Jake said. "Just a small team. Fast. Quiet." He knelt and set the rig on the stone. A flickering green map bloomed upward.

"Here. Shadow Ridge. Varun marked it before he—"

He stopped.

"A day's trek," Harun said grimly. "Spirits avoid that place."

"That's why Malik chose it," Jake replied. "He thinks no one will follow."

"Who goes with you?" Kori asked.

"Two fast warriors. One who knows the ridge. And someone who understands the old bindings." Jake met her eyes. "If Varun twisted them, only you can unmake it."

Kori's face tightened. "You ask me to clean blood from my own legacy."

"I'm asking you to honor it."

Elder Nahi rose. "I oppose sending an elder."

Kori lifted her staff. The tap echoed once.

"Then our ways bend—or they break."

Two warriors stepped forward—Naru, vigilant and calm, and Rak-ka, broad-shouldered and scarred. They bowed.

Jake nodded once—then turned and walked out.

Outside, the night air struck him sharp and cold. Jake paced the forest path to the cliff's edge, boots crunching leaves. The valley stretched below, dark and endless. Doubt gnawed at him. What if he led them wrong? What if this was all his fault?

The wind tugged at his clothes. He stared at the horizon until footsteps approached behind him.

"Jake," Amna called softly.

He turned. Tharik stood with her, Naru and Rakka close.

"You can't go alone," Tharik said. "Not this time."

"I need to prepare," Jake said.

"And you will," Amna replied. "With us."

Jake exhaled. "I just want to fix it. I don't want anyone else paying for my mistakes."

Rakka shook his head. "You already carry enough."

Amna stepped closer. "You don't lose strength by letting us help."

Jake studied their faces, the resolve there. At last, he nodded.

"Alright. But we do this right."

Relief crossed Amna's face.

"We move at dawn," Naru said. "North trail. Less traveled."

They turned back together.

Later, as the elders regrouped, Kori came to Jake's side.

"It's settled," she said. "We depart at first light."

Jake studied the map etched into stone. The beacon on his rig pulsed once, uneven.

"This isn't just about stopping Malik," he murmured. "It's about pulling time back from the brink."

Above them, the torches guttered.

The cavern exhaled.

As preparations for the strike began, an uneasy silence settled over the cavern. Outside, dawn had not yet broken, but the camp stirred with hushed whispers and torchlight. Leather straps creaked as packs were cinched. Time felt heavy—each minute stretched thin, each second ticking in time with the rift's pulse.

Jake stood at the cave mouth, outlined by pale blue pre-dawn light. Behind him, Kori, Naru, and Rakka finished their checks. The air held what didn't need saying.

Amna stepped from a side passage, her eyes bright with resolve. There was reassurance there, too, and Jake felt it steady him.

"We've got your back," she said, calm and certain.

He turned, a small smile breaking through. "I know."

"You know what I mean." Her gaze slid from the rig at his shoulder to the horizon, where the ground gave a faint, arrhythmic shiver. "If something happens to you out there—"

He met her eyes. The space between them tightened, words hanging unfinished. Disbelief crossed her face, then settled into a careful nod as she accepted what he didn't say. It felt like a hinge moment—quiet, irreversible.

"No crowns for me," she said, shaking her head with a thin smile. "Don't hand me one I didn't ask for."

"Neither did I," Jake said.

They stood together as the stars thinned toward morning. Jake's fingers brushed the stone disc at his throat. Emma's necklace was warm—too warm—alive with the rift's rhythm.

For a heartbeat, the warmth stuttered—like a skipped pulse—followed by a thin, metallic whisper that didn't belong to wind or stone.

"You've changed," Amna said softly. "When you first arrived, you were all noise. Now... you're a pattern."

"What changed?"

"Emma," he said. "Even when she's not here, she's why I keep moving."

Amna nodded. "Then find your way home."

A scout emerged from the lower path. "The ridge trail's clear. No sign of Malik's patrols."

Jake turned back to the group. Naru tightened her bowstring. Rakka grunted as he set his spear. Kori, exhausted but unbent, waited.

"We move light," Jake said. "No fires. No noise."

"No noise?" Kori echoed.

"They're listening," Jake replied. "I don't know how—but they are."

At his belt, the rig gave a brief, wrong chirrup—flat, synthetic, not one of his alerts—then went dark again. Jake stilled. Amna felt it too.

They moved. Shapes dissolved into mist beyond the cave.

Amna stayed.

She watched until the last outline vanished, then pressed her palm to the stone to steady herself. Her breath hitched once—harder than she meant it to—and she swallowed it down. Leaving him was the cost she chose, and it hurt more than any wound.

When she finally turned back into the cavern, the silence closed behind her like a door.

Chapter 18: Fall of the Tyrant

The cave trembled once more, a deep, resonant shiver that rolled through stone as dawn's first light crept over the horizon. Jake braced near the fire, fingers locked around the moss-wrapped bench as if he could keep the world still by force.

Beside him, Elder Kori and the others were still catching their breath from their hurried return after the ground had lurched beneath them outside. Most of the tribe had retreated deeper into the inner caverns—some sleeping in fitful knots, others whispering prayers meant for older things than fear. Only sentries and elders remained up, moving through the passages with careful, practiced quiet.

Beyond the cave entrance, wind whistled through shattered trees. Shadows stitched themselves across the limestone walls in time with the flames. Charred wood and damp fur hung in the air, a blunt reminder of homes lost and dangers that hadn't moved on just because the sky was lightening.

A few moments later, Tharik burst into the cavern, face drawn tight as storm cloud. Dirt streaked his hands. He held a bundle of ash bark wrapped hard and fast, the bindings marked with blood.

"I found this at the edge of the forest," he said, voice rough with cold and haste.

Jake pushed to his feet as Amna stepped closer, jaw set. "What kind of message?"

Tharik exhaled; his breath fogged and vanished. "The ridge shuddered under me—barely at first, like stone breathing. Then it surged. I followed it downhill, past cracked roots and splintered brush. That's when I found this."

He unfurled the bark with care. In the center lay a spiral, roughly carved but deliberate, a broken hourglass etched within its coils. The symbol didn't glow, not really, yet Jake's skin prickled as if it did. As if it had learned his name and was testing the shape of it.

Elder Kori limped forward, bone-and-feathered walker tapping softly. She squinted, fingers grazing the grooves.

"It's a summons," she said. "Malik knows the rift has opened. And he's calling for a meeting—with you."

Jake's gaze dropped to the fire. The flames snapped and leapt, restless. His hand curled without thinking, fingertips brushing the hilt of The Bridge at his side, warm against his ribs like a small, steady heart.

"He wants me alone."

Amna stepped into his path. "You're not going."

Jake didn't answer at first. The spiral tightened behind his eyes each time he breathed. The fire hissed; the wind slipped deeper into the cave's throat, nosing at the edges of their warmth.

"If we're going to fix this..." The words sat heavy on his tongue, like iron. "...I have to face him."

Amna's stare didn't soften.

Jake lifted his chin. "But I won't do it alone."

He looked at her, then Tharik, then Elder Kori—three points of a compass he'd come to trust more than his own sense of north.

"You," he said to Amna. "Tharik. Elder Kori. You come with me."

Elder Kori inclined her head, saying nothing yet.

Jake forced his voice steady. "I won't move without your counsel. If there's another way, I'll take it." He glanced once more at the bark, at the broken hourglass inside the spiral. "But if there isn't—will you stand with me?"

Silence settled, thick with thought. Then Elder Kori nodded, slow as a tide turning.

"Then let the wheel turn," she said. "Let the tide speak."

They emerged into the clearing later that morning, where trees grew sparse and frost clung to stone like pale lichen. Mist pooled low across the ground, thick and silver under the first true light.

Atop the rise, Malik stood alone.

Two guards waited behind him at a respectful distance, still as cut obsidian. His blade hung at his side—black as night, threaded with faint red veins that glinted like banked embers.

Before Jake could move, Tharik stepped ahead, spear angled low but firm. He swept his gaze along the tree line and jagged rocks beyond, watching for the smallest twitch of shape or shadow.

"Wait," Tharik murmured. "Let me see if he's truly alone."

Jake nodded once, throat tight.

Tharik advanced, steps quiet and sure, like a ritual already halfway spoken. He stopped within speaking distance, voice clear and edged.

"You called for a meeting. But are you truly alone, Malik? Or do your shadows hide more than the wind?"

Malik's answer came slowly, as if hauled up from deep in his chest. "They left after the screams rose from your caves. After Varun came back smoking—half-shadow, half-man." His mouth tightened. "My warriors scattered. Said I walked with omens. Said I was cursed."

Tharik studied him, breath a slow cloud. Then he turned back. "He's alone."

Only then did Jake move forward. The Bridge lay warm and steady against his ribs, humming faintly—as if it recognized the air around Malik, as if something nearby answered it.

Amna and Tharik flanked him. Elder Kori stood tall despite the gnarled staff in her hand, bone feathers whispering with each small shift of wind.

Malik's voice carried, low and even. "You. The ghost time keeps coughing back up."

Jake didn't flinch. "Then stop trying to erase me."

Malik tilted his head. Light caught in the red veins of his blade. "You carry something unnatural. That cursed glowing stick of yours..." His gaze pinned The Bridge as if he could see through Jake's skin to it. "It dreams while you sleep. It remembers futures that never happened."

Elder Kori stepped forward, and the clearing seemed to tighten around her presence. "Does it guide you," she asked, voice quiet and sharp, "or do you bleed its visions into the world?"

For a moment something shifted in Malik's eyes—recognition, regret, a memory refusing to die.

"I bleed dreams," he said, softer. "Sometimes I wake choking on futures that don't belong to me."

The trees rustled though no wind moved them. Mist curled at their feet. Heat pressed briefly against Jake's skin, not from the sun, not from the fire he'd left behind, but from something layered and unfinished—timelines brushing like cloth in the dark.

Jake took another step. "You're not the end," he said. "You're the doorway. The rift is bigger than either of us."

Malik didn't answer. His grip shifted, almost imperceptible, as if he'd felt the same truth and hated it.

Jake's mind flashed to Kori's earlier lessons, to the way the tribe measured strength: not by how much blood you spilled, but by what you were willing to carry afterward.

He glanced at the others, then back at Malik. "Let time choose," Jake said. "Not tricks. Not your blade's whispers." He lifted his chin toward Tharik. "You want the tribe? Then face him. The old way."

The air changed. Tharik blinked once, then straightened as if a spine of iron slid into place. Elder Kori's expression barely moved, but her approval was there, a small shift in the set of her mouth. Amna's breath caught; Jake felt it at his shoulder like a held flame.

Malik looked at the hunter, and for the first time his stance changed—not toward aggression, but toward weight. Toward acceptance of an old, sacred burden.

Tharik raised his spear in answer, jaw set.

"A duel?" Malik asked, voice barely above the hush of windless trees.

Tharik nodded once. "You called for it."

Malik's eyes closed briefly, as if offering something—prayer, apology, or surrender—to the ground beneath him.

"So be it," he said.

The sky dulled from blue to a flat gray, as if the day itself refused to watch too brightly. Stones marked the arena's edge, half-buried in frost, each one worn by older circles and older outcomes. No one shouted. Even the birds seemed to have gone quiet.

Tharik and Malik faced each other under the twisted branches of a dead pine. Frost crunched beneath their feet with every shift of weight. Jake stood at the boundary, fingers hovering near The Bridge, every nerve tuned hard and high. The device's warmth felt steady, patient, like a hand on the back of his neck.

Malik moved first.

He came down in a vicious arc meant to break bone through guard. Tharik rolled, the blade shearing air where his head had been. The spear snapped up on the rebound, quick as thought, its tip scoring Malik's ribs. Blood beaded dark against pale morning.

A sound rippled through the trees—not wind, not leaves, but feet. People emerging. Survivors from the caves. Elders with staffs. Warriors with torn wraps and soot in their hair. They didn't need to be called. The duel called them. They gathered behind the stones, forming a tight, unbroken ring, faces hard with grief and hunger, eyes bright with something that might have been hope if they dared name it.

Malik's fury sharpened. He swept low, blade skimming for Tharik's legs. Tharik blocked with the haft, but the edge kissed flesh anyway, biting into his thigh. Blood spattered against stone, black-red against frost.

Tharik grunted, breath ragged for a beat, then steadied. He did not go down.

Jake's pulse hammered. The Bridge hummed once, then again, not louder, not frantic—attentive. Jake watched Malik's footwork, the repetition in his shoulders, the way every third strike leaned into the same rhythm. Pattern. Habit. The kind of thing a man clung to when his mind was full of screaming futures.

"Break the pattern," Jake whispered, barely sound.

Tharik's eyes flicked toward him for a heartbeat—acknowledgment, not dependence. Then Tharik shifted his weight as if to commit left.

Malik bit.

He lunged, overextended, hungry for the finish. Tharik turned it into empty air, a feint that stole Malik's balance. The spear drove up and in, catching Malik's shoulder with a wet, decisive punch of impact. Malik staggered back, boots skidding, then dropped to one knee, breath heaving, blade tip scraping frost.

The ring of watchers held still, as if the entire clearing had inhaled and forgotten how to exhale.

Malik lifted his head, eyes cutting past Tharik to Jake, confusion and rage tangled tight. "Do you think this matters?" he spat. "A circle of stones. An old game."

Jake stepped forward to the boundary, careful not to break it. "You were never the real threat," he said. His voice didn't rise, but it carried. "You were the first crack. The rift started with you." He glanced at the mist, at the way it gathered behind Malik like a curtain waiting for a hand. "But it doesn't end with you."

Malik's mouth twisted, ready for a retort—

—and the ground trembled.

Not the deep quake from the night before. Smaller. Closer. Like something under the skin of the world flexing, impatient. The crowd flinched as one. Mist behind Malik parted in a clean, unnatural line, and for a heartbeat the rift glowed: vast, patient, listening.

The Bridge warmed against Jake's ribs, threads of green light stirring as if it had found a rhythm to match.

Malik's footing shifted. He reached for purchase that wasn't there. His expression cracked from anger into something bare and human.

Fear.

He pitched backward as if yanked, not by gravity but by a pull with intention. Elder Kori lifted her staff, bone feathers trembling.

"The weapon is still," she declared, voice ringing through the hush. "The spiral ends here."

Malik's hand clawed at the air. Then the rift took him.

No warning flicker. No stutter of light like Varun. One breath he existed, bleeding and furious. The next there was only emptiness where he had been, and the air went cold with the sudden absence. The rift sealed itself with a sound like a sigh swallowed.

No one spoke. The circle held, stunned into stillness by the clean finality of it.

Jake stared at The Bridge.

SYNC STABILITY: 100% — PORTAL ANCHOR STABLE

Its pulse steadied. Green threads rose into the air, aligning with the earth's rhythm as if the world had finally decided on a single beat.

Amna stood beside him, voice thin with disbelief. "It held?"

Jake nodded slowly. "It held. The path is open." His throat worked around the words he'd been afraid to believe. "Stable enough to go home."

He exhaled, eyes scanning the mist-soft horizon as if Emma might step out of it. "Emma set things up," he said, quieter. "She sent the parts back before everything fractured. Without her, we wouldn't have seen the disruption in time."

"Varun," Amna said. Then, after a beat: "Malik."

Jake nodded once. "They interfered with the signal. Distorted the rift." He looked to the place where Malik had vanished, where the air still felt wrong. "But it's clear now."

He turned toward the mist, where time whispered like a memory you couldn't quite hold.

Not the end.

Not yet.

Chapter 19: The Parting Glass

T he sun was a sliver on the horizon, light retreating like a fighter giving ground. Only hours had passed since Malik vanished, yet the village moved as if days had been laid on its shoulders. Smoke clung low. Torches guttered stubbornly against the dark, their light catching on huts scarred by panic and flight.

A breeze worried the dust at Jake's feet, carrying smoldered wood and crushed herbs—burn and balm together. He stood where torchlight thinned into the tree line, the village behind him and the wild ahead.

In his pocket, the necklace Amna had given him lay still. The stone disc no longer vibrated, but it held warmth from days against his skin, as if it remembered his pulse and refused to forget it.

Amna stepped into the torchlight. Her voice stayed steady; her eyes didn't bother pretending.

"You were never meant to stay," she said.

Jake lifted his gaze. "I don't know that I was meant to leave, either."

The village watched from shadow and doorway, quiet in that way that wasn't peace, only attention. Elders were already gathering near the fire circle, gifts in hand, faces solemn with ceremony.

Amna's mouth tried for a wry smile. It made it halfway and faltered. Her cloak shifted in the breeze; her braid had loosened, strands escaping like they'd had enough of being held.

"Time doesn't care what we're meant for," she said. "It only cares that it moves."

He nodded. The rig sat strapped tight across his chest, lights dim but steady, a patient heartbeat. In a moment it would wake the vortex again. It had synced with the necklace at dawn, when the anomaly in the southern ruins flared and the ground's wrongness rose up through his boots.

Amna had only given him one detail then, close to his ear, as if saying it louder might make it real.

"Runes," she had whispered. "Carved into the stone."

That was enough. The rest had announced itself in Jake's blood: the rig's sudden hunger for signal, the stone disc in his pocket slamming awake, the certainty settling behind his ribs like a locked door.

The portal wasn't closed. Not yet. But it would be. Soon.

"I've done what I can here," Jake said, voice rougher than he meant. "But the anomalies are getting worse. If I stay—"

"You'll fracture everything," Amna finished.

He didn't ask how she knew. Somehow she always landed on the truth without reaching for it.

Behind them, torches sputtered harder. The air tightened, charged, as if the forest itself held its breath.

The villagers stood beyond the fire circle, silent. Curiosity on some faces, fear on others, and under it all the same question: what does it mean when a doorway opens and doesn't want to close?

One by one, the elders stepped forward.

Elder Daro approached with his carved staff, tapping it once against the ground. "Jake of the storm light," he said, "you walk into a river few have dared to touch. May your mind be clear and your memory sharp."

Elder Muna pressed a small bundle of dried herbs into Jake's palm. The stems crackled softly. "A token for courage," she said, "in case your world forgets to offer it."

Then Elder Kori stepped into the torchlight, wrapped in her ceremonial cloak. The murmur of the village thinned until there was only her and the night listening.

"You are a thread now," she said. Her voice was deep, unhurried, and it made the words feel older than speech. "Woven into a tapestry older than you can name. You can't undo your place in it—only honor it."

Jake's throat tightened. He bowed his head, not to surrender, but to accept the weight.

"Go with the memory of who you were," Kori continued, "and return with the wisdom of who you've become."

"Thank you," Jake managed, the words small and honest.

Amna stood apart, arms folded as if she could hold herself together by force. For a moment she hesitated, fingers worrying the edge of her cloak. Then she stepped close enough that Jake felt her warmth cut through the cold.

Her hand slipped into his pocket.

Jake startled. "Amna—"

She drew out the stone disc—the one she had given him—and for a heartbeat it sat in her palm like a captured ember. Her other hand unfolded a frayed scrap of cloth from within her cloak, careful as if unwrapping a wound. Inside lay a different necklace: finer chain, older metal, a shape that tugged at Jake's memory like a hook.

Emma's.

Jake blinked, mind skidding. "But—"

"I gave you mine," Amna said softly, and her fingers closed around the stone disc. "But this one was never mine to keep."

The necklace caught torchlight and returned it in a thin, steady shimmer. Amna stepped closer and lifted the chain toward Jake's neck. Her hands shook once, barely.

"It's time," she said.

He didn't move away. He couldn't.

She fastened it behind his neck with gentle care, as if this final act could be made painless by tenderness. When her eyes met his, the farewell passed between them without words: a whole history compressed into a single look.

Jake's chest ached at the thought of Emma—his little sister—somewhere in the life he'd left. Maybe she was still in his room. Maybe she was pacing holes into the floor. Maybe she'd already learned how to live with missing pieces.

"She came for me," he murmured. Gratitude and grief braided tight inside him.

Amna nodded. "Not recently." Her voice softened further. "It's been decades, by my guess. She didn't speak of what she ran from. Only what she needed to find."

The idea of Emma alone in this world twisted something in him. He wanted to rewind every wrong turn, gather her up, drag her back through time with his own hands.

"She was like you," Amna said. "Sharp. Curious." Her gaze flicked to the necklace now resting against his collarbone. "But different, too. Like she already knew how it would end."

A low rumble moved through the distance, too deep for thunder. The wind shifted. The air took on that strange pressure Jake had come to recognize—time flexing, waking.

The vortex was calling.

"I have to go," Jake whispered, almost to himself.

Amna's breath hitched. She steadied it. "The necklace..." she said. "She told me it was meant to remind someone who they were. In case they forgot."

Jake touched the metal at his throat. It was cool now, but it carried heat in its center, like a coal that refused to die.

"I won't forget," he said.

Amna stepped in until their foreheads nearly touched. Her voice cracked at last. "Then promise me. Promise me you'll remember us. That it mattered. That we mattered."

Jake closed his eyes. The village, the cave, the firelight, the way her hands had felt on his neck—he pressed it all into the place memory lived.

"I promise."

From the village heart, drumbeats began again—faint and steady, a rhythm meant to anchor what the world kept trying to tear loose.

Jake opened his eyes. "You were the best part of this place," he said. "I'll carry that. Always."

Amna's smile returned, and this time it held. "Then go."

He hesitated only once more, then turned and walked away.

The clearing behind the village no longer felt like a clearing. It felt like a wound.

In its center churned the portal—electric, unstable—a jagged tear in the air that made Jake's teeth ache. Above it, the sky pulsed with light that didn't belong to any sun. The runes around it glowed in a wide circle, ancient cuts filled with a modern, hungry radiance.

Jake stepped up to the edge, heart hammering. Emma's necklace hummed against his chest, answering the vortex like a tuning fork.

He raised The Bridge. The screen stuttered with static, then steadied. Numbers spilled down the display in tight, urgent cascades—energy spikes, drift warnings, a countdown that made his stomach drop. The portal's outer rim wavered like torn paper in a storm.

He breathed once, hard, and moved.

Hands moving with urgency, he keyed commands, recalibrated the signal, tightened the anchor. The Bridge warmed beneath his grip. The rig across his chest pulsed in sync with the necklace, as if all three were finally speaking the same language.

Soft footsteps behind him.

Amna.

She stood at the edge of the rune circle, near stones that had begun to sweat heat. Jake kept his eyes on the readouts another second, because looking at her felt like inviting the moment to break him.

"I never told you what the runes meant," she said.

He glanced back, forcing something lighter into his voice because if he didn't, the fear would show too plainly. "Let me guess. 'Danger: unstable time rift ahead'?"

A soft chuckle escaped her. "No." She nodded toward the glowing circle. "They say, 'Return what was taken.'"

Jake turned back to the vortex. The words slid into place with everything else he'd learned here, fitting too neatly to be coincidence.

"Sounds about right," he said.

He swallowed. "You should go. It's not safe."

"So should you," Amna replied, and there was no heat in it—only truth.

Jake let out a breath that shook on the way out. "I'm scared," he admitted.

"I know."

"Not just of what's waiting on the other side." His voice thinned. "But of what I'm leaving behind."

"I know that, too."

Silence settled between them, heavy with everything they couldn't fix. The vortex's pull deepened, the sound rising into a low roar that thrummed in Jake's bones. The runes brightened, then dimmed, like a slow blink.

Jake straightened. He needed to ask it, even if the answer didn't change anything.

"Will you be okay?"

Amna tilted her head, expression unreadable for a heartbeat. Then she spoke with the steadiness she'd used to keep other people from falling apart.

"We were never meant to be safe," she said. "But we will endure."

Jake managed a small smile, the kind you wore when you had no armor left except humor. "That sounds like something Emma would say."

"It's something my father always said," Amna answered, a ghost of a smile on her mouth.

The vortex surged, colors twisting into a violent, beautiful storm. Jake took one step closer.

Amna lifted her hand—not a wave, not a formal farewell. Just an acknowledgment, plain as breath: I'm here. I saw you. I won't pretend this wasn't real.

Jake looked at her one last time. Fear and certainty braided tight in his chest.

Then he stepped into the storm.

Color swallowed him.

Sound, too—metallic and distant, like a thousand forks struck at once. Jake tumbled through a tunnel of fractured moments: Emma laughing, torchlight on Amna's cheek, the spiral symbol burning behind his eyes. The Bridge in his grip stuttered, glitched, then caught again, pulling itself into alignment as if refusing to lose him now.

Time tightened. Twisted. Let go.

He hit the floor hard.

Pain bloomed through his ribs and shoulder, sharp and clean. Dust lifted in a slow cloud. Jake blinked grit from his lashes and stared up at the lazy spin of his ceiling fan.

His room.

His lab.

Familiar and wrong at the same time, air dry and thick with the old ozone bite he associated with sleepless nights and solder and mistakes he didn't want to admit.

He sucked in a ragged breath and sat up, palms flat on the floor to steady the world. The necklace at his throat lay cold against his skin—Emma's chain, undeniable weight, undeniable proof.

The door burst open.

Emma stood there, eyes wide, breath caught between terror and relief. "Jake?!"

He got to his feet just as she crossed the room in two strides and slammed into him. Her arms locked around his waist like she could keep him from vanishing again by sheer force.

"I thought I lost you," she choked.

Jake held her, eyes burning. He breathed her in—shampoo, laundry soap, home.

"I made it back," he said, voice barely there.

Emma pulled back enough to see him, hands still fisted in his shirt. Her gaze dropped to his neck. Confusion sharpened through the relief.

"Is that... my necklace?"

Jake's throat tightened. He touched the chain, fingers trembling.

"Yes," he said. "It's yours."

Emma's hand rose, hovering, then she cupped the pendant like she was afraid it might disappear. Her eyes searched his face, trying to measure time by what it had done to him. Just days before, she had realized the necklace was missing, right after Jake had vanished.

"How long?" she whispered. "Jake, how long were you gone?"

Jake swallowed. The answer sat in his mouth like something too large to speak all at once.

"I don't know yet," he admitted. "Not the way you mean." He looked past her, as if he could see the other world through drywall and stale air. "But I know this—someone kept it safe. People who had no reason to... and did anyway."

Emma's brows drew together. "People?"

Jake tightened his grip on The Bridge, still in his hand, as if he might slip again if he let go. The screen was dark now, quiet, but the weight of it felt different—less like a tool, more like a promise.

"I've got a story to tell," he said.

Emma stared at him, shaking slightly, and nodded once.

In the small room full of dust and old hums, with her hands still on the necklace at his throat, Jake felt the truth settle in: coming back wasn't the end.

It was the beginning.

Chapter 20: Horizon's Edge

Midnight stains the windowpanes cobalt, turning Jake Parker's bedroom-lab into a shallow aquarium of neon. Monitors line the far wall like vigilant moons, their edges pulsing out of sync in blues and greens. The air tastes of flux and burnt plastic. A bowl of stale cereal petrifies atop a stack of quantum-physics journals, forgotten mid-thought.

Under everything hums Waltham's quiet suburban night. Soft tires on pavement. A distant train's long, hollow note. In here, though, the universe has narrowed to a single object on the workbench.

The Bridge.

Sleek. Quiet. Certain.

Its polished casing catches the monitor glow in thin ribbons. Along its rim, digital runes rotate with a slow inevitability, not flashing so much as measuring. Like a clock that doesn't tick, only decides.

Jake stands in front of it, eyes bright behind slightly crooked glasses, fingers twitching with the old, dangerous anticipation that has never once asked permission.

"This is it," he murmurs. "Old failures, new rules."

He lays his palm on the cool panel. The Bridge answers with a subtle pulse, a shift in tone. LEDs chase in sequence, clean and deliberate. On the main screen, the interface unfurls: the familiar diagnostic lattice, but sharper now. No jitter at the edges. No stutter in the timing graph. A line that used to spike and collapse holds steady in green.

He exhales through his nose, almost a laugh. "No drift."

His eyes close anyway.

Failure rushes up first: fried circuits, dead signals, nights of static and stubborn pride. Then something else pushes in behind it, uninvited. Not data. Not code.

Smoke.

Not the burnt-plastic kind. Wood-smoke. Damp fur. Torchlight trembling against stone. A pressure in the air like the world holding its breath.

Jake opens his eyes, throat tight, and looks down at the bench beside the workbench clutter.

The necklace.

Emma's chain, older than it should be, catching monitor light and returning it as a thin shimmer. The pendant's stone disc holds a faint warmth, as if it remembers being pressed to a different chest. His memory supplies the rest in flashes he can't file: cold dawn, the hiss of a portal, Amna's hands steady at his collar, her voice cracking on a promise.

He turns the pendant once between his fingers. The warmth is real. The rest, he tells himself, is just what happens when you survive something that shouldn't exist.

He refocuses on The Bridge.

He doesn't need to tell himself what it has become. He can see it in the way the room seems to arrange itself around it. The old scavenged guts are gone, replaced with graphene coils seated cleanly in the casing. Symbols scroll across the interface, part code and part something he refuses to name. He doesn't translate them anymore. He feels their intent, the way you feel a current through water.

Jake runs his thumb along a fresh seam in the casing, half admiring, half afraid. Every upgrade has demanded more power, more heat, more risk. Every gain has shaved seconds off the countdown that still mutters at the edge of his sleep.

A warning chime breaks the midnight hush, low and resonant.

New data spools into view.

TEMPORAL SHEAR: SPIKE DETECTED

ANCHOR VARIANCE: 0.03% (RISING)

Coordinates resolve into a tight cluster, deep beneath the ruins, deeper than the last flare. The numbers settle like a verdict.

Jake swears, quiet and sharp.

So it's not done. Of course it isn't. The Bridge was never a lifeline. It's a compass, and it keeps pointing straight at the next fracture.

Decision time, Parker.

He snaps the casing closed, the sound too loud in the still room. The rig goes over his shoulder. He checks the pulse torch charge by habit. The weight settles into his muscles like readiness.

He looks once more at the necklace, then hooks it carefully around his own throat, letting the pendant rest against his sternum. The stone cools, then warms again, a small insistence.

"System," he says, voice steady now. "Confirm integration. Confirm anchor stability."

Green text streams across the main screen, clean and immediate:

INTEGRATION COMPLETE.

ANCHOR CALIBRATION: STABLE.

DRIFT COMPENSATION: ACTIVE.

Jake sinks into his chair for a single breath. The familiar creak grounds him. He scans the monitors. All green. For once, everything holds.

He's been close before. Close enough to taste victory and have it collapse into static. This time the code doesn't resist. It moves in rhythm, as if the machine has finally agreed to speak his language.

"The upgrade was a risk," he says, mostly to himself. "But it's the only way the next jump doesn't tear me apart."

He stands. No extra ritual. No delay disguised as preparation.

His palm settles on the command node.

The Bridge stirs. Lights deepen from cold blue toward a warmer hue that makes the shadows feel older. The coils answer with a low hum that rises through the workbench and into his bones. The air thickens, threaded with that pressure again, not quite electrical, not quite memory, but close enough to both to make his skin prickle.

He doesn't picture chaos. He refuses it.

He pictures a clean shift. A doorway held open with intention.

"All those failures," he murmurs, fingers hovering over the control array, "were input. Data points."

Doubt still waits at the edge of his mind. Systems overloading. Promises collapsing. The sickening drop when reality refuses to co-operate. But the code has never lied. It has only demanded exactness, and Jake has bled for that lesson long enough to earn it.

"Activate," he says.

The response is crisp, immediate:

ACTIVATION PROTOCOL INITIATED.

Runes brighten along the rim. The monitors pulse in time with the rising hum. Shadows slide across circuit boards and notebooks and the fossilized remains of old obsessions, as if the room is being re-written around a single decision.

Jake catches his reflection in one dark monitor: fear in his eyes, hope under it, resolve finally aligned. He touches the pendant once, a small anchor against his skin.

"This time," he whispers, "I make the rules."

Epilogue: Threads of Fate

In Jake's cluttered bedroom, the low hum of electronics and the papery rustle of scattered notes formed a familiar symphony. Crumpled schematics littered the floor. LEDs blinked in restless cycles, throwing thin, nervous shadows. A soldering iron still smoked faintly on the desk's edge, as if he'd set it down mid-thought and never looked back.

Jake stood in the chaos with Emma's stone necklace in his hand. The pendant was smooth and round, etched with spiral markings that caught the monitor light and returned it in deep, cobalt flashes. It didn't shine so much as answer, a soft resonance under his skin that made the hair on his arms lift.

His gaze shifted to The Bridge.

It rested on the desk in its newly fashioned frame, calm as if calm were a choice. A sentinel waiting for orders. Sleek casing. Clean seams. A quiet hum that didn't belong to any fan or coil he'd ever built before.

It had brought him back.

And with it came the things his room couldn't hold: Tharik's blunt warnings, Elder Kori's riddles that landed like stones in water, Amna's quiet defiance. Ritual braided into machine logic. Smoke in stone corridors. A sky split open and wrong.

The main monitor blipped.

Erratic. Then sharp.

Jake leaned in, breath caught. Cascading code froze midstream, then vanished like it had been erased by a stronger hand. In its place, blazing white text flared across the dark screen:

COORDINATE LOCK — ANCIENT GREECE

The words pulsed once, twice, not quite a heartbeat, more like a signal insisting on being seen.

"This can't be right," he breathed.

In his palm, the necklace tremored, subtle enough that anyone else would have missed it. Jake didn't. The vibration matched the portal's rhythm from the day he left, the same pressure behind the sternum, the same low insistence in the bones.

A beacon.

A door.

He spun to the desk and snatched up his worn notebook. Its pages were packed with scrawled symbology, glitch traces, portal frequency maps. Every anomaly logged. Every impossible event pinned down with numbers and stubbornness.

This was it.

"It's real," he whispered. "Again."

The air thickened, not with heat but with density, as if the room itself had gained weight. The monitor's glow brightened until the whites threatened to wash out the edges of everything else.

Jake typed commands, fast, trying to isolate the source. He traced the signature line by line, expecting a location, a vector, a point in space.

But the signal didn't resolve into a place.

It resolved into a when.

Then the door burst open.

Emma.

Backpack slung over one shoulder. Shoes tied tight. Determination radiating off her so hard it felt like a second light source. Her eyes locked on the screen and didn't blink.

"So it's true," she said. "I thought I felt something."

Jake stared at her, the ground under his certainty shifting. "You're... ready?"

Emma nodded and dropped the pack at her feet. "I've been packed since the day you came back."

"You didn't come with me last time," Jake said. "Not really. A version of you found me, yeah, but—"

"I know." Her voice trembled, not with fear, but with force. "That's why I'm going this time."

He opened his mouth. She didn't let him hide behind words.

"I remember the necklace glowing," Emma said. "I remember the way you came back different." She stepped closer, gaze flicking to The Bridge the way people look at a weapon. "And I saw how you held that thing, like it was the only tether you had."

Jake looked down, jaw tight, and said nothing. The silence was admission enough.

Emma moved to stand beside him, shoulder close but not touching. Not crowding. Just there.

"Whatever this is," she said, quieter now, "you're not doing it alone."

Jake's breath eased out of him in a slow line. "The signal's strong," he said. "Stronger than before. It's not just calling me anymore."

The screen flashed again, harsh and bright:

EVENT CONVERGENCE: IMMINENT

Emma's voice softened. "It's her, isn't it?"

Jake's fingers tightened around the notebook. His thumb brushed the spiral on the pendant. "The Emma from the past," he said. "She left this behind. Told the tribe to wait for me." He swallowed. "I don't know how she got there first. Or how she knew me. But she did."

Emma stared at the text like it might rearrange itself into something kinder. "Then maybe this is her way of bringing us together," she said. "Both versions of me. Both versions of you."

Jake let out a short, sharp laugh. "That's terrifying."

Emma's mouth curved. "But it's time."

She nudged her backpack closer to The Bridge. "So. What do we do?"

Jake scanned the room: blueprints, translations, ancient rubbings, failed runs, forgotten code. Evidence of a life that used to fit inside these walls.

He tightened the strap on the rig. "We go prepared," he said. "This isn't the same portal. It's Ancient Greece, but the stream's warped." He tapped the monitor with two fingers. "The return path won't match the way out."

He held the necklace out to Emma.

She took it carefully, as if it could bruise. She slipped the chain over her head and settled the pendant at her collarbone with reverence, the spiral centered like an eye.

Emma nodded once. "Then we don't mess it up."

A silence bloomed between them, full of everything they weren't saying.

Then Emma asked, "What about Mom and Dad?"

Jake hesitated, and the hesitation was its own answer. "They'll think we're at school," he said. "Or camping. Or something."

Emma's brows lifted. "You're trusting me to lie to them?"

He grinned, quick and bright. "We're already breaking time. Might as well break curfew."

She huffed a laugh. "Besides," Jake added, "how long was I gone last time?"

"A couple of days," Emma said, grin widening. "Didn't even know you left."

A tone sounded from the rig, crisp and wrong in the familiar room. The screen pulsed. The air shifted, pressure building like the breath before a storm.

TEMPORAL ANCHOR DETECTED — INITIALIZING

Emma's spine straightened. "It's happening."

Jake's hands flew over the keys. "The vortex is forming on its own," he said. "The necklace is syncing with the rig. Feedback loop's triggering the jump."

Emma's fingers brushed the pendant. It was glowing now, faint but growing, the cobalt deepening until it looked like the inside of a bruise.

The room vibrated. Wires whispered as the pitch rose. Dust lifted from the floorboards in a slow, startled halo.

Jake turned to her, the question he couldn't stop himself from asking in his eyes. "You really want to do this?"

"No one's meant to watch from the sidelines," Emma said. "You told me that."

He smiled, and it hurt. "Then suit up."

He moved fast: locking coordinates, syncing biometric keys, adjusting for multi-user transfer. The rig pulsed in layered cycles, responding not just to him, but to them both. The monitors dimmed.

Sparks snapped behind the console. The air tasted metallic, like lightning getting ready.

Then—

The portal erupted into being.

A ring of compressed light. A roar that didn't travel through air so much as through time. The walls seemed to flex inward. The ceiling rippled, as if the room were being seen through water.

Emma flinched, but she held her ground.

"Hold on!" Jake shouted.

He grabbed her hand as the floor buckled and the ring widened, licking at the edge of reality. Her eyes shone, not with fear, but awe. The pendant at her throat pulsed in lockstep with The Bridge's hum.

They locked eyes.

Hope. Trust.

Then the pressure snapped into motion.

Time folded, clean and violent, and the bedroom-lab blinked out around them.

AFTERWORD

When I first imagined Jake Parker, I saw a teenager standing on the edge of time—with a backpack full of code, a heart full of questions, and absolutely no idea what he was about to set in motion.

Jake the Time Jumper: The Portal Walker is more than a time-travel adventure. It's a story about memory, loss, wonder, and the terrifying freedom of second chances. Jake didn't ask to be a hero. He didn't even know what kind of story he was in. But like many of us, he jumped anyway—half-ready, fully afraid, and driven by hope.

This book began with a single question: What if the future needed saving, not from destruction, but from forgetting?

And so, Jake jumped.

From ancient tribes and fractured timelines to whispered legends and glowing relics, this is just the start of his journey. And Emma's. And yours.

Jake the Time Jumper is Book One of the The Portal Walker series. The next chapter will push Jake further— into a warped vision of **Ancient Greece**, where history's echoes are louder, the stakes sharper, and the truths harder to bear. If you felt the tremor of time beneath your feet, if you caught a glimpse of your own choices in Jake's—then thank you for walking with him. With me. With all of us trying to make sense of the past to shape what comes next.

And if you loved the ride, please consider leaving a review or sharing this story with a fellow traveler. Every word you pass on gives this story new life—and helps me keep building more worlds worth jumping into.

With endless gratitude across all timelines,

— *A.D.□ Tenebris*

Author of The Portal Walker Series

THANK YOU FOR READING!

Hey, Adventurers—

I'm **A.D. Tenebris**, and I'm thrilled you joined me for this journey. If the story sparked your curiosity, made you laugh, or kept you up way past midnight (sorry□–□not sorry), I'd love to hear what you thought. A quick review does more than you know: it helps fellow readers decide to take the plunge and lets this book find its tribe.

Got sixty seconds?

Drop a rating or a few honest lines wherever you picked up the book. Your voice keeps these pages turning for new readers.

Stay in the loop

Want more spice, speed, and supernatural secrets? Sign up for my newsletter at https://adtenebris.com/mailing-list and get a FREE copy of *The Wingman Chronicles!* Join the squad for exclusive updates, behind-the-scenes extras, and first looks at upcoming releases. Don't miss out—your next adventure starts with one click!

Sign up here: https://adtenebris.com/mailing-list

Let's connect

- Instagram: behind-the-scenes sketches, mood boards, and occasional time-travel memes.

- BlueSky: rapid-fire writing vids, character polls, and live Q&As.

- Website: (friendly platform): bite-sized lore drops and sneak peeks.

Pick your spot, say hi, and tell me which character is you favorite. Until the next adventure—keep questioning reality, embrace the impossible, and read fearlessly.

— A.D. Tenebris

ABOUT THE AUTHOR

A.D. Tenebris writes where memory fractures and myth bleeds into the present.

Blending science fiction, fantasy, and echoes of ancient worlds, his stories explore the unseen threads that bind time, truth, and identity. From time-bending odysseys to divine rebellions and post-apocalyptic awakenings, his work 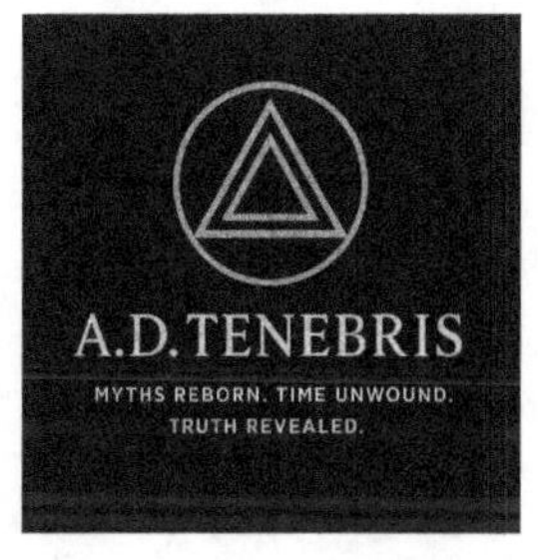

delves into the spaces between—between light and shadow, fate and free will, legacy and loss.

Tenebris is known for crafting immersive worlds and emotionally charged narratives driven by flawed heroes, forgotten histories, and impossible choices. His young adult and crossover novels are read by those who crave high-concept adventure wrapped in heart and mystery.

When not bending timelines or mythologizing the future, he writes under stars, studies the past, and believes every story we tell is a bridge to the one we're becoming.

www.ingramcontent.com/pod-product-compliance
Lightning Source LLC
Chambersburg PA
CBHW060410310726

48976CB00003B/1008